Diana Of The Crossways Book 2

by

George Meredith

Diana Of The Crossways Book 2
by George Meredith

Copyright © 2023

ISBN: 978-93-57484-99-2

Published by

DOUBLE 9 BOOKS

2/13-B, Ansari Road
Daryaganj, New Delhi – 110002
info@double9books.com
www.double9books.com
Tel. 011-40042856

This book is under public domain

ABOUT THE AUTHOR

George Meredith OM (February 12, 1828-May 18, 1909) was born in Portsmouth, United Kingdom. He was an English poet, writer, and author, whose books are noted for their intelligence, extraordinary dialogues, and aphoristic way of writing. Meredith's books are also recognised for psychological studies of character and a highly subjective perspective on life that is a long way ahead of its time, considering women are equals to men in all streams. His most popular works are The Ordeal of Richard Feverel (1859) and The Egoist (1879). He was nominated for the Nobel Prize in Literature seven times.

CONTENTS

CHAPTER IX.
SHOWS HOW A POSITION OF DELICACY FOR A LADY AND GENTLEMAN WAS MET IN SIMPLE FASHION WITHOUT HURT TO EITHER

Redworth's impulse was to laugh for very gladness of heart, as he proffered excuses for his tremendous alarums and in doing so, the worthy gentleman imagined he must have persisted in clamouring for admission because he suspected, that if at home, she would require a violent summons to betray herself. It was necessary to him to follow his abashed sagacity up to the mark of his happy animation.

'Had I known it was you!' said Diana, bidding him enter the passage. She wore a black silk mantilla and was warmly covered.

She called to her maid Danvers, whom Redworth remembered: a firm woman of about forty, wrapped, like her mistress, in head-covering, cloak, scarf and shawl. Telling her to scour the kitchen for firewood, Diana led into a sitting-room. 'I need not ask—you have come from Lady Dunstane,' she said. 'Is she well?'

'She is deeply anxious.'

'You are cold. Empty houses are colder than out of doors. You shall soon have a fire.'

She begged him to be seated.

The small glow of candle-light made her dark rich colouring orange in shadow.

'House and grounds are open to a tenant,' she resumed. 'I say good-bye to them to-morrow morning. The old couple who are in charge sleep in the village to-night. I did not want them here. You have quitted the Government service, I think?'

'A year or so since.'

'When did you return from America?'

'Two days back.'

'And paid your visit to Copsley immediately?'

'As early as I could.'

'That was true friendliness. You have a letter for me?'

'I have.'

He put his hand to his pocket for the letter.

'Presently,' she said. She divined the contents, and nursed her resolution to withstand them. Danvers had brought firewood and coal. Orders were given to her, and in spite of the opposition of the maid and intervention of the gentleman, Diana knelt at the grate, observing:

'Allow me to do this. I can lay and light a fire.'

He was obliged to look on: she was a woman who spoke her meaning. She knelt, handling paper, firewood and matches, like a housemaid. Danvers proceeded on her mission, and Redworth eyed Diana in the first fire-glow. He could have imagined a Madonna on an old black Spanish canvas.

The act of service was beautiful in gracefulness, and her simplicity in doing the work touched it spiritually. He thought, as she knelt there, that never had he seen how lovely and how charged with mystery her features were; the dark large eyes full on the brows; the proud line of a straight nose in right measure to the bow of the lips; reposeful red lips, shut, and their curve of the slumber-smile at the corners. Her forehead was broad; the chin of a sufficient firmness to sustain: that noble square; the brows marked by a soft thick brush to the temples; her black hair plainly drawn along her head to the knot, revealed by the mantilla fallen on her neck.

Elegant in plainness, the classic poet would have said of her hair and dress. She was of the women whose wits are quick in everything they do. That which was proper to her position, complexion, and the hour, surely marked her appearance. Unaccountably this night, the fair fleshly presence over-weighted her intellectual distinction, to an observer bent on vindicating her innocence. Or rather, he saw the hidden in the visible.

Owner of such a woman, and to lose her! Redworth pitied the husband.

The crackling flames reddened her whole person. Gazing, he remembered Lady Dunstane saying of her once, that in anger she had the nostrils of a war-horse. The nostrils now were faintly alive under some sensitive impression of her musings. The olive cheeks, pale as she stood in the doorway, were flushed by the fire-beams, though no longer with their swarthy central rose, tropic flower of a pure and abounding blood, as it had seemed. She was now beset by battle. His pity for her, and his eager championship, overwhelmed the spirit of compassion for the foolish wretched husband. Dolt, the man must be, Redworth thought; and he asked inwardly, Did the miserable tyrant suppose of a woman like this, that she would be content to shine as a candle in a grated lanthorn? The generosity of men speculating upon other men's possessions is known. Yet the man who loves a woman has to the full the husband's jealousy of her good name. And a lover, that without the claims of the alliance, can be wounded on her behalf, is less distracted in his homage by the personal luminary, to which man's manufacture of balm and incense is mainly drawn when his love is wounded. That contemplation of her incomparable beauty, with the multitude of his ideas fluttering round it, did somewhat shake the personal luminary in Redworth. He was conscious of pangs. The question bit him: How far had she been indiscreet or wilful? and the bite of it was a keen acid to his nerves. A woman doubted by her husband, is always, and even to her champions in the first hours of the noxious rumour, until they had solidified in confidence through service, a creature of the wilds, marked for our ancient running. Nay, more than a cynical world, these latter will be sensible of it. The doubt casts her forth, the general yelp drags her down; she runs like the prey of the forest under spotting branches; clear if we can think so, but it has to be thought in devotedness: her character is abroad. Redworth bore a strong resemblance to, his fellowmen, except for his power of faith in this woman. Nevertheless it required the superbness of her beauty and the contrasting charm of her humble posture of kneeling by the fire, to set him on his right track of mind. He knew and was sure of her. He dispersed the unhallowed fry in attendance upon any stirring of the reptile part of us, to look at her with the eyes of a friend. And if . . . !—a little mouse of a thought scampered out of one of the chambers of his head and darted along the passages, fetching a sweat to his brows. Well, whatsoever the fact, his heart was hers! He hoped he could be charitable to women.

She rose from her knees and said: 'Now, please, give me the letter.'

He was entreated to excuse her for consigning him to firelight when she left the room.

Danvers brought in a dismal tallow candle, remarking that her mistress had not expected visitors: her mistress had nothing but tea and bread and butter to offer him. Danvers uttered no complaint of her sufferings; happy in being the picture of them. 'I'm not hungry,' said he.

A plate of Andrew Hedger's own would not have tempted him. The foolish frizzle of bacon sang in his ears as he walked from end to end of the room; an illusion of his fancy pricked by a frost-edged appetite. But the anticipated contest with Diana checked and numbed the craving.

Was Warwick a man to proceed to extremities on a mad suspicion?—What kind of proof had he?

Redworth summoned the portrait of Mr. Warwick before him, and beheld a sweeping of close eyes in cloud, a long upper lip in cloud; the rest of him was all cloud. As usual with these conjurations of a face, the index of the nature conceived by him displayed itself, and no more; but he took it for the whole physiognomy, and pronounced of the husband thus delineated, that those close eyes of the long upper lip would both suspect and proceed madly.

He was invited by Danvers to enter the dining-room.

There Diana joined him.

'The best of a dinner on bread and butter is, that one is ready for supper soon after it,' she said, swimming to the tea-tray. 'You have dined?'

'At the inn,' he replied.

'The Three Ravens! When my father's guests from London flooded The Crossways, The Three Ravens provided the overflow with beds. On nights like this I have got up and scraped the frost from my window-panes to see them step into the old fly, singing some song of his. The inn had a good reputation for hospitality in those days. I hope they treated you well?'

'Excellently,' said Redworth, taking an enormous mouthful, while his heart sank to see that she who smiled to encourage his eating had been weeping. But she also consumed her bread and butter.

'That poor maid of mine is an instance of a woman able to do things against the grain,' she said. 'Danvers is a foster-child of luxury. She loves it; great houses, plentiful meals, and the crowd of twinkling footmen's calves. Yet you see her here in a desolate house, consenting to cold, and I know not what, terrors of ghosts! poor soul. I have some mysterious attraction for her. She would not let me come alone. I should have had to hire some old Storling grannam, or retain the tattling keepers of the house. She loves her native country too, and disdains the foreigner. My tea you may trust.'

Redworth had not a doubt of it. He was becoming a tea-taster. The merit of warmth pertained to the beverage. 'I think you get your tea from Scoppin's, in the City,' he said.

That was the warehouse for Mrs. Warwick's tea. They conversed of Teas; the black, the green, the mixtures; each thinking of the attack to come, and the defence. Meantime, the cut bread and butter having flown, Redwerth attacked the loaf. He apologized.

'Oh! pay me a practical compliment,' Diana said, and looked really happy at his unfeigned relish of her simple fare.

She had given him one opportunity in speaking of her maid's love of native country. But it came too early.

'They say that bread and butter is fattening,' he remarked.

'You preserve the mean,' said she.

He admitted that his health was good. For some little time, to his vexation at the absurdity, she kept him talking of himself. So flowing was she, and so sweet the motion of her mouth in utterance, that he followed her lead, and he said odd things and corrected them. He had to describe his ride to her.

'Yes! the view of the Downs from Dewhurst,' she exclaimed. 'Or any point along the ridge. Emma and I once drove there in Summer, with clotted cream from her dairy, and we bought fresh-plucked wortleberries, and stewed them in a hollow of the furzes, and ate them with ground biscuits and the clotted cream iced, and thought it a luncheon for seraphs. Then you dropped to the road round under the sand-heights—and meditated railways!'

'Just a notion or two.'

'You have been very successful in America?'

'Successful; perhaps; we exclude extremes in our calculations of the still problematical.'

'I am sure,' said she, 'you always have faith in your calculations.'

Her innocent archness dealt him a stab sharper than any he had known since the day of his hearing of her engagement. He muttered of his calculations being human; he was as much of a fool as other men—more!

'Oh! no,' said she.

'Positively.'

'I cannot think it.'

'I know it.'

'Mr. Redworth, you will never persuade me to believe it.'

He knocked a rising groan on the head, and rejoined 'I hope I may not have to say so to-night.'

Diana felt the edge of the dart. 'And meditating railways, you scored our poor land of herds and flocks; and night fell, and the moon sprang up, and on you came. It was clever of you to find your way by the moonbeams.'

'That's about the one thing I seem fit for!'

'But what delusion is this, in the mind of a man succeeding in everything he does!' cried Diana, curious despite her wariness. 'Is there to be the revelation of a hairshirt ultimately?—a Journal of Confessions? You succeeded in everything you aimed at, and broke your heart over one chance miss?'

'My heart is not of the stuff to break,' he said, and laughed off her fortuitous thrust straight into it. 'Another cup, yes. I came . . .'

'By night,' said she, 'and cleverly found your way, and dined at The Three Ravens, and walked to The Crossways, and met no ghosts.'

'On the contrary—or at least I saw a couple.'

'Tell me of them; we breed them here. We sell them periodically to the newspapers!'

'Well, I started them in their natal locality. I saw them, going down the churchyard, and bellowed after them with all my lungs. I wanted directions to The Crossways; I had missed my way at some turning. In an instant they were vapour.'

Diana smiled. 'It was indeed a voice to startle delicate apparitions! So do roar Hyrcanean tigers. Pyramus and Thisbe—slaying lions! One of your ghosts carried a loaf of bread, and dropped it in fright; one carried a pound of fresh butter for home consumption. They were in the churchyard for one in passing to kneel at her father's grave and kiss his tombstone.'

She bowed her head, forgetful of her guard.

The pause presented an opening. Redworth left his chair and walked to the mantelpiece. It was easier to him to speak, not facing her.

'You have read Lady Dunstane's letter,' he began.

She nodded. 'I have.'

'Can you resist her appeal to you?'

'I must.'

'She is not in a condition to bear it well. You will pardon me, Mrs. Warwick . . .'

'Fully! Fully!'

'I venture to offer merely practical advice. You have thought of it all, but have not felt it. In these cases, the one thing to do is to make a stand. Lady Dunstane has a clear head. She sees what has to be endured by you. Consider: she appeals to me to bring you her letter. Would she have chosen me, or any man, for her messenger, if it had not appeared to her a matter of life and death? You count me among your friends.'

'One of the truest.'

'Here are two, then, and your own good sense. For I do not believe it to be a question of courage.'

'He has commenced. Let him carry it out,' said Diana.

Her desperation could have added the cry—And give me freedom! That was the secret in her heart. She had struck on the hope for the detested yoke to be broken at any cost.

'I decline to meet his charges. I despise them. If my friends have faith in me—and they may!—I want nothing more.'

'Well, I won't talk commonplaces about the world,' said Redworth. 'We can none of us afford to have it against us. Consider a moment: to your friends you are the Diana Merion they knew, and they will not suffer an injury to your good name without a struggle. But if you fly? You leave the dearest you have to the whole brunt of it.'

'They will, if they love me.'

'They will. But think of the shock to her. Lady Dunstane reads you—'

'Not quite. No, not if she even wishes me to stay!' said Diana.

He was too intent on his pleading to perceive a signification.

'She reads you as clearly in the dark as if you were present with her.'

'Oh! why am I not ten years older!' Diana cried, and tried to face round to him, and stopped paralyzed. 'Ten years older, I could discuss my situation, as an old woman of the world, and use my wits to defend myself.'

'And then you would not dream of flight before it!'

'No, she does not read me: no! She saw that I might come to The Crossways. She—no one but myself can see the wisdom of my holding aloof, in contempt of this baseness.'

'And of allowing her to sink under that which your presence would arrest. Her strength will not support it.'

'Emma! Oh, cruel!' Diana sprang up to give play to her limbs. She dropped on another chair. 'Go I must, I cannot turn back. She saw my old attachment to this place. It was not difficult to guess . . . Who but I can see the wisest course for me!'

'It comes to this, that the blow aimed at you in your absence will strike her, and mortally,' said Redworth.

'Then I say it is terrible to have a friend,' said Diana, with her bosom heaving.

'Friendship, I fancy, means one heart between two.'

His unstressed observation hit a bell in her head, and set it reverberating. She and Emma had spoken, written, the very words. She drew forth her Emma's letter from under her left breast, and read some half-blinded lines.

Redworth immediately prepared to leave her to her feelings— trustier guides than her judgement in this crisis.

'Adieu, for the night, Mrs. Warwick,' he said, and was guilty of eulogizing the judgement he thought erratic for the moment. 'Night is a calm adviser. Let me presume to come again in the morning. I dare not go back without you.'

She looked up. As they faced together each saw that the other had passed through a furnace, scorching enough to him, though hers was the delicacy exposed. The reflection had its weight with her during the night.

'Danvers is getting ready a bed for you; she is airing linen,' Diana, said. But the bed was declined, and the hospitality was not pressed. The offer of it seemed to him significant of an unwary cordiality and thoughtlessness of tattlers that might account possibly for many things— supposing a fool or madman, or malignants, to interpret them.

'Then, good night,' said she.

They joined hands. He exacted no promise that she would be present in the morning to receive him; and it was a consolation to her desire for freedom, until she reflected on the perfect confidence it implied, and felt as a quivering butterfly impalpably pinned.

CHAPTER X.
THE CONFLICT OF THE NIGHT

Her brain was a steam-wheel throughout the night; everything that could be thought of was tossed, nothing grasped.

The unfriendliness of the friends who sought to retain her recurred. For look—to fly could not be interpreted as a flight. It was but a stepping aside, a disdain of defending herself, and a wrapping herself in her dignity. Women would be with her. She called on the noblest of them to justify the course she chose, and they did, in an almost audible murmur.

And O the rich reward. A black archway-gate swung open to the glittering fields of freedom.

Emma was not of the chorus. Emma meditated as an invalid. How often had Emma bewailed to her that the most, grievous burden of her malady was her fatal tendency to brood sickly upon human complications! She could not see the blessedness of the prospect of freedom to a woman abominably yoked. What if a miserable woman were dragged through mire to reach it! Married, the mire was her portion, whatever she might do. That man—but pass him!

And that other—the dear, the kind, careless, high-hearted old friend. He could honestly protest his guiltlessness, and would smilingly leave the case to go its ways. Of this she was sure, that her decision and her pleasure would be his. They were tied to the stake. She had already tasted some of the mortal agony. Did it matter whether the flames consumed her?

Reflecting on the interview with Redworth, though she had performed her part in it placidly, her skin burned. It was the beginning of tortures if she stayed in England.

By staying to defend herself she forfeited her attitude of dignity and lost all chance of her reward. And name the sort of world it is, dear friends, for which we are to sacrifice our one hope of freedom, that we may preserve our fair fame in it!

Diana cried aloud, 'My freedom!' feeling as a butterfly flown out of a box to stretches of sunny earth beneath spacious heavens. Her bitter marriage, joyless in all its chapters, indefensible where the man was right as well as where insensately wrong, had been imprisonment. She excused him down to his last madness, if only the bonds were broken. Here, too, in this very house of her happiness with her father, she had bound herself to the man voluntarily, quite inexplicably. Voluntarily, as we say. But there must be a spell upon us at times. Upon young women there certainly is.

The wild brain of Diana, armed by her later enlightenment as to the laws of life and nature, dashed in revolt at the laws of the world when she thought of the forces, natural and social, urging young women to marry and be bound to the end.

It should be a spotless world which is thus ruthless.

But were the world impeccable it would behave more generously.

The world is ruthless, dear friends, because the world is hypocrite! The world cannot afford to be magnanimous, or even just.

Her dissensions with her husband, their differences of opinion, and puny wranglings, hoistings of two standards, reconciliations for the sake of decency, breaches of the truce, and his detested meanness, the man behind the mask; and glimpses of herself too, the half-known, half-suspected, developing creature claiming to be Diana, and unlike her dreamed Diana, deformed by marriage, irritable, acerb, rebellious, constantly justifiable against him, but not in her own mind, and therefore accusing him of the double crime of provoking her and perverting her—these were the troops defiling through her head while she did battle with the hypocrite world.

One painful sting was caused by the feeling that she could have loved— whom? An ideal. Had he, the imagined but unvisioned, been her yoke- fellow, would she now lie raising caged-beast cries in execration of the yoke? She would not now be seeing herself as hare, serpent, tigress! The hypothesis was reviewed in negatives: she had barely a sense of softness, just a single little heave of the bosom, quivering upward and leadenly sinking, when she glanced at a married Diana heartily mated. The regrets of the youthful for a life sailing away under medical sentence of death in the sad eyes of relatives resemble it. She could have loved. Good-bye to that!

A woman's brutallest tussle with the world was upon her. She was in the arena of the savage claws, flung there by the man who of all others should have protected her from them. And what had she done to deserve it? She listened to the advocate pleading her case; she primed him to admit the charges, to say the worst, in contempt of legal prudence, and thereby expose her transparent honesty. The very things awakening a mad suspicion proved her innocence. But was she this utterly simple person? Oh, no! She was the Diana of the pride in her power of fencing with evil—by no means of the order of those ninny young women who realize the popular conception of the purely innocent. She had fenced and kept her guard. Of this it was her angry glory to have the knowledge. But she had been compelled to fence. Such are men in the world of facts, that when a woman steps out of her domestic tangle to assert, because it is a tangle, her rights to partial independence, they sight her for their prey, or at least they complacently suppose her accessible. Wretched at home, a woman ought to bury herself in her wretchedness, else may she be assured that not the cleverest, wariest guard will cover her character.

Against the husband her cause was triumphant. Against herself she decided not to plead it, for this reason, that the preceding Court, which was the public and only positive one, had entirely and justly exonerated her. But the holding of her hand by the friend half a minute too long for friendship, and the over-friendliness of looks, letters, frequency of visits, would speak within her. She had a darting view of her husband's estimation of them in his present mood. She quenched it; they were trifles, things that women of the world have to combat. The revelation to a fair-minded young woman of the majority of men being naught other than men, and some of the friendliest of men betraying confidence under the excuse of temptation, is one of the shocks to simplicity which leave her the alternative of misanthropy or philosophy. Diana had not the heart to hate her kind, so she resigned herself to pardon, and to the recognition of the state of duel between the sexes-active enough in her sphere of society. The circle hummed with it; many lived for it. Could she pretend to ignore it? Her personal experience might have instigated a less clear and less intrepid nature to take advantage of the opportunity for playing the popular innocent, who runs about with astonished eyes to find herself in so hunting a world, and wins general compassion, if not shelter in unsuspected and unlicenced places. There is perpetually the inducement to act the hypocrite before the hypocrite world, unless a woman submits to be the humbly knitting housewife, unquestioningly worshipful of her lord; for the world is ever gracious to an hypocrisy that pays homage to the mask of virtue by copying it; the world is hostile to the face of an innocence not conventionally simpering and quite surprised; the world prefers decorum to honesty. 'Let me be myself, whatever the martyrdom!' she cried, in that phase of young sensation when, to the blooming woman; the putting on of a mask appears to wither her and reduce her to the show she parades. Yet, in common with her sisterhood, she owned she had worn a sort of mask; the world demands it of them as the price of their station. That she had never worn it consentingly, was the plea for now casting it off altogether, showing herself as she was, accepting martyrdom, becoming the first martyr of the modern woman's cause—a grand position! and one imaginable to an excited mind in the dark, which does not conjure a critical humour, as light does, to correct the feverish sublimity. She was, then, this martyr, a woman capable of telling the world she knew it, and of, confessing that she had behaved in disdain of its rigider rules, according to her own ideas of her immunities. O brave!

But was she holding the position by flight? It involved the challenge of consequences, not an evasion of them.

She moaned; her mental steam-wheel stopped; fatigue brought sleep.

She had sensationally led her rebellious wits to The Crossways, distilling much poison from thoughts on the way; and there, for the luxury of a still seeming indecision, she sank into oblivion.

CHAPTER XI.
RECOUNTS THE JOURNEY IN A CHARIOT, WITH A CERTAIN AMOUNT OF DIALOGUE, AND A SMALL INCIDENT ON THE ROAD

In the morning the fight was over. She looked at the signpost of The Crossways whilst dressing, and submitted to follow, obediently as a puppet, the road recommended by friends, though a voice within, that she took for the intimations of her reason, protested that they were wrong, that they were judging of her case in the general, and unwisely — disastrously for her.

The mistaking of her desires for her reasons was peculiar to her situation.

'So I suppose I shall some day see The Crossways again,' she said, to conceive a compensation in the abandonment of freedom. The night's red vision of martyrdom was reserved to console her secretly, among the unopened lockers in her treasury of thoughts. It helped to sustain her; and she was too conscious of things necessary for her sustainment to bring it to the light of day and examine it. She had a pitiful bit of pleasure in the gratification she imparted to Danvers, by informing her that the journey of the day was backward to Copsley.

'If I may venture to say so, ma'am, I am very glad,' said her maid.

'You must be prepared for the questions of lawyers, Danvers.'

'Oh, ma'am! they'll get nothing out of me, and their wigs won't frighten me.'

'It is usually their baldness that is most frightening, my poor Danvers.'

'Nor their baldness, ma'am,' said the literal maid; 'I never cared for their heads, or them. I've been in a Case before.'

'Indeed!' exclaimed her mistress; and she had a chill.

Danvers mentioned a notorious Case, adding, 'They got nothing out of me.'

'In my Case you will please to speak the truth,' said Diana, and beheld in the looking-glass the primming of her maid's mouth. The sight shot a sting.

'Understand that there is to be no hesitation about telling the truth of what you know of me,' said Diana; and the answer was, 'No, ma'am.'

For Danvers could remark to herself that she knew little, and was not a person to hesitate. She was a maid of the world, with the quality of faithfulness, by nature, to a good mistress.

Redworth's further difficulties were confined to the hiring of a conveyance for the travellers, and hot-water bottles, together with a postillion not addicted to drunkenness. He procured a posting-chariot, an ancient and musty, of a late autumnal yellow unrefreshed by paint; the only bottles to be had were Dutch Schiedam. His postillion, inspected at Storling, carried the flag of habitual inebriation on his nose, and he deemed it adviseable to ride the mare in accompaniment as far as Riddlehurst, notwithstanding the postillion's vows upon his honour that he was no drinker. The emphasis, to a gentleman acquainted with his countrymen, was not reassuring. He had hopes of enlisting a trustier fellow at Riddlehurst, but he was disappointed; and while debating upon what to do, for he shrank from leaving two women to the conduct of that inflamed troughsnout, Brisby, despatched to Storling by an afterthought of Lady Dunstane's, rushed out of the Riddlehurst inn taproom, and relieved him of the charge of the mare. He was accommodated with a seat on a stool in the chariot. 'My triumphal car,' said his captive. She was very amusing about her postillion; Danvers had to beg pardon for laughing. 'You are happy,' observed her mistress. But Redworth laughed too, and he could not boast of any happiness beyond the temporary satisfaction, nor could she who sprang the laughter boast of that little. She said to herself, in the midst of the hilarity, 'Wherever I go now, in all weathers, I am perfectly naked!' And remembering her readings of a certain wonderful old quarto book in her father's library, by an eccentric old Scottish nobleman, wherein the wearing of garments and sleeping in houses is accused as the cause of human degeneracy, she took a forced merry stand on her return to the primitive healthful state of man and woman, and affected scorn of our modern ways of dressing and thinking. Whence it came that she had some of her wildest seizures of iridescent humour. Danvers attributed the fun to her mistress's gladness in not having pursued her bent to quit the country. Redworth saw deeper, and was nevertheless amazed by the airy hawk-poise and pounce-down of her wit, as she ranged high and low, now capriciously generalizing, now dropping bolt upon things of passage—the postillion jogging from rum to gin, the rustics baconly agape, the horse-kneed ostlers. She touched them to the life in similes and phrases; and next she was aloft, derisively philosophizing, but with a comic afflatus that dispersed the sharpness of her irony in mocking laughter. The afternoon refreshments at the inn of the county market-town, and the English idea of public hospitality, as to manner and the substance provided for wayfarers, were among the themes she made memorable to him. She spoke of everything tolerantly, just naming it in a simple sentence, that fell with a ring and chimed: their host's ready acquiescence in receiving, orders, his contemptuous disclaimer of stuff he did not keep, his flat indifference to the sheep he sheared, and the phantom half-crown flickering in one eye of the anticipatory waiter; the pervading and confounding smell of stale beer over all the apartments; the prevalent, notion of bread, butter, tea, milk, sugar, as matter for the exercise of a native inventive genius—these were reviewed in quips of metaphor.

'Come, we can do better at an inn or two known to me,' said Redworth.

'Surely this is the best that can be done for us, when we strike them with the magic wand of a postillion?' said she.

'It depends, as elsewhere, on the individuals entertaining us.'

'Yet you admit that your railways are rapidly "polishing off" the individual.'

'They will spread the metropolitan idea of comfort.'

'I fear they will feed us on nothing but that big word. It booms— a curfew bell—for every poor little light that we would read by.'

Seeing their beacon-nosed postillion preparing too mount and failing in his jump, Redworth was apprehensive, and questioned the fellow concerning potation.

'Lord, sir, they call me half a horse, but I can't 'bids water,'' was the reply, with the assurance that he had not 'taken a pailful.'

Habit enabled him to gain his seat.

'It seems to us unnecessary to heap on coal when the chimney is afire; but he may know the proper course,' Diana said, convulsing Danvers; and there was discernibly to Redworth, under the influence of her phrases, a likeness of the flaming 'half-horse,' with the animals all smoking in the frost, to a railway engine. 'Your wrinkled centaur,' she named the man. Of course he had to play second to her, and not unwillingly; but he reflected passingly on the instinctive push of her rich and sparkling voluble fancy to the initiative, which women do not like in a woman, and men prefer to distantly admire. English women and men feel toward the quick-witted of their species as to aliens, having the demerits of aliens-wordiness, vanity, obscurity, shallowness, an empty glitter, the sin of posturing. A quick-witted woman exerting her wit is both a foreigner and potentially a criminal. She is incandescent to a breath of rumour. It accounted for her having detractors; a heavy counterpoise to her enthusiastic friends. It might account for her husband's discontent- the reduction of him to a state of mere masculine antagonism. What is the husband of a vanward woman? He feels himself but a diminished man. The English husband of a voluble woman relapses into a dreary mute. Ah, for the choice of places! Redworth would have yielded her the loquent lead for the smallest of the privileges due to him who now rejected all, except the public scourging of her. The conviction was in his mind that the husband of this woman sought rather to punish than be rid of her. But a part of his own emotion went to form the judgement.

Furthermore, Lady Dunstane's allusion to her 'enemies' made him set down her growing crops of backbiters to the trick she had of ridiculing things English. If the English do it themselves, it is in a professionally robust, a jocose, kindly way, always with a glance at the other things, great things, they excel in; and it is done to have the credit of doing it. They are keen to catch an inimical tone; they will find occasion to chastise the presumptuous individual, unless it be the leader of a party, therefore a power; for they respect a power. Redworth knew their quaintnesses; without overlooking them he winced at the acid of an irony that seemed to spring from aversion, and regretted it, for her sake. He had to recollect that she was in a sharp-strung mood, bitterly surexcited; moreover he reminded himself of her many and memorable phrases of enthusiasm for England—Shakespeareland, as she would sometimes perversely term it, to sink the country in the poet. English fortitude, English integrity, the English disposition to do justice to dependents, adolescent English ingenuousness, she was always ready to laud. Only her enthusiasm required rousing by circumstances; it was less at the brim than her satire. Hence she made enemies among a placable people.

He felt that he could have helped her under happier conditions. The beautiful vision she had been on the night of the Irish Ball swept before him, and he looked at her, smiling.

'Why do you smile?' she said.

'I was thinking of Mr. Sullivan Smith.'

'Ah! my dear compatriot! And think, too, of Lord Larrian.'

She caught her breath. Instead of recreation, the names brought on a fit of sadness. It deepened; shy neither smiled nor rattled any more. She gazed across the hedgeways at the white meadows and bare-twigged copses showing their last leaves in the frost.

'I remember your words: "Observation is the most, enduring of the pleasures of life"; and so I have found it,' she said. There was a brightness along her under-eyelids that caused him to look away.

The expected catastrophe occurred on the descent of a cutting in the sand, where their cordial postillion at a trot bumped the chariot against the sturdy wheels of a waggon, which sent it reclining for support upon a beech-tree's huge intertwisted serpent roots, amid strips of brown bracken and pendant weeds, while he exhibited one short stump of leg, all boot, in air. No one was hurt. Diana disengaged herself from the shoulder of Danvers, and mildly said:

'That reminds me, I forgot to ask why we came in a chariot.'

Redworth was excited on her behalf, but the broken glass had done no damage, nor had Danvers fainted. The remark was unintelligible to him, apart from the comforting it had been designed to give. He jumped out, and held a hand for them to do the same. 'I never foresaw an event more positively,' said he.

'And it was nothing but a back view that inspired you all the way,' said Diana.

A waggoner held the horses, another assisted Redworth to right the chariot. The postillion had hastily recovered possession of his official seat, that he might as soon as possible feel himself again where he was most intelligent, and was gay in stupidity, indifferent to what happened behind him. Diana heard him counselling the waggoner as to the common sense of meeting small accidents with a cheerful soul.

'Lord!' he cried, 'I been pitched a Somerset in my time, and taken up for dead, and that didn't beat me!'

Disasters of the present kind could hardly affect such a veteran. But he was painfully disconcerted by Redworth's determination not to entrust the ladies any farther to his guidance. Danvers had implored for permission to walk the mile to the town, and thence take a fly to Copsley. Her mistress rather sided with the postillion; who begged them to spare him the disgrace of riding in and delivering a box at the Red Lion.

'What'll they say? And they know Arthur Dance well there,' he groaned. 'What! Arthur! chariotin' a box! And me a better man to his work now than I been for many a long season, fit for double the journey! A bit of a shake always braces me up. I could read a newspaper right off, small print and all. Come along, sir, and hand the ladies in.'

Danvers vowed her thanks to Mr. Redworth for refusing. They walked ahead; the postillion communicated his mixture of professional and human feelings to the waggoners, and walked his horses in the rear, meditating on the weak-heartedness of gentryfolk, and the means for escaping being chaffed out of his boots at the Old Red Lion, where he was to eat, drink, and sleep that night. Ladies might be fearsome after a bit of a shake; he would not have supposed it of a gentleman. He jogged himself into an arithmetic of the number of nips of liquor he had taken to soothe him on the road, in spite of the gentleman. 'For some of 'em are sworn enemies of poor men, as yonder one, ne'er a doubt.'

Diana enjoyed her walk beneath the lingering brown-red of the frosty November sunset, with the scent of sand-earth strong in the air.

'I had to hire a chariot because there was no two-horse carriage,' said Redworth, 'and I wished to reach Copsley as early as possible.'

She replied, smiling, that accidents were fated. As a certain marriage had been! The comparison forced itself on her reflections.

'But this is quite an adventure,' said she, reanimated by the brisker flow of her blood. 'We ought really to be thankful for it, in days when nothing happens.'

Redworth accused her of getting that idea from the perusal of romances.

'Yes, our lives require compression, like romances, to be interesting, and we object to the process,' she said. 'Real happiness is a state of dulness. When we taste it consciously it becomes mortal—a thing of the Seasons. But I like my walk. How long these November sunsets burn, and what hues they have! There is a scientific reason, only don't tell it me. Now I understand why you always used to choose your holidays in November.'

She thrilled him with her friendly recollection of his customs.

'As to happiness, the looking forward is happiness,' he remarked.

'Oh, the looking back! back!' she cried.

'Forward! that is life.'

'And backward, death, if you will; and still at is happiness. Death, and our postillion!'

'Ay; I wonder why the fellow hangs to the rear,' said Redworth, turning about.

'It's his cunning strategy, poor creature, so that he may be thought to have delivered us at the head of the town, for us to make a purchase or two, if we go to the inn on foot,' said Diana. 'We 'll let the manoeuvre succeed.'

Redworth declared that she had a head for everything, and she was flattered to hear him.

So passing from the southern into the western road, they saw the town- lights beneath an amber sky burning out sombrely over the woods of Copsley, and entered the town, the postillion following.

CHAPTER XII.
BETWEEN EMMA AND DIANA

Diana was in the arms of her friend at a late hour of the evening, and Danvers breathed the amiable atmosphere of footmen once more, professing herself perished. This maid of the world, who could endure hardships and loss of society for the mistress to whom she was attached, no sooner saw herself surrounded by the comforts befitting her station, than she indulged in the luxury of a wailful dejectedness, the better to appreciate them. She was unaffectedly astonished to find her outcries against the cold and the journeyings to and fro interpreted as a serving- woman's muffled comments on her mistress's behaviour. Lady Dunstane's maid Bartlett, and Mrs. Bridges the housekeeper, and Foster the butler, contrived to let her know that they could speak an if they would; and they expressed their pity of her to assist her to begin the speaking. She bowed in acceptance of Fosters offer of a glass of wine after supper, but treated him and the other two immediately as though they had been interrogating bigwigs.

'They wormed nothing out of me,' she said to her mistress at night, undressing her. 'But what a set they are! They've got such comfortable places, they've all their days and hours for talk of the doings of their superiors. They read the vilest of those town papers, and they put their two and two together of what is happening in and about. And not one of the footmen thinks of staying, because it 's so dull; and they and the maids object—did one ever hear?—to the three uppers retiring, when they 've done dining, to the private room to dessert.'

'That is the custom?' observed her mistress.

'Foster carries the decanter, ma'am, and Mrs. Bridges the biscuits, and Bartlett the plate of fruit, and they march out in order.'

'The man at the head of the procession, probably.'

'Oh yes. And the others, though they have everything except the wine and dessert, don't like it. When I was here last they were new, and hadn't a word against it. Now they say it's invidious! Lady Dunstane will be left without an under-servant at Copsley soon. I was asked about your boxes, ma'am, and the moment I said they were at Dover, that instant all three peeped. They let out a mouse to me. They do love to talk!'

Her mistress could have added, 'And you too, my good Danvers!' trustworthy though she knew the creature to be in the main.

'Now go, and be sure you have bedclothes enough before you drop asleep,' she said; and Danvers directed her steps to gossip with Bartlett.

Diana wrapped herself in a dressing-gown Lady Dunstane had sent her, and sat by the fire, thinking of the powder of tattle stored in servants' halls to explode beneath her: and but for her choice of roads she might have been among strangers. The liking of strangers best is a curious exemplification of innocence.

'Yes, I was in a muse,' she said, raising her head to Emma, whom she expected and sat armed to meet, unaccountably iron-nerved. 'I was questioning whether I could be quite as blameless as I fancy, if I sit and shiver to be in England. You will tell me I have taken the right road. I doubt it. But the road is taken, and here I am. But any road that leads me to you is homeward, my darling!' She tried to melt, determining to be at least open with her.

'I have not praised you enough for coming,' said Emma, when they had embraced again.

'Praise a little your "truest friend of women." Your letter gave the tug. I might have resisted it.'

'He came straight from heaven! But, cruel Tony where is your love?'

'It is unequal to yours, dear, I see. I could have wrestled with anything abstract and distant, from being certain. But here I am.'

'But, my own dear girl, you never could have allowed this infamous charge to be undefended?'

'I think so. I've an odd apathy as to my character; rather like death, when one dreams of flying the soul. What does it matter? I should have left the flies and wasps to worry a corpse. And then-good-bye gentility! I should have worked for my bread. I had thoughts of

America. I fancy I can write; and Americans, one hears, are gentle to women.'

'Ah, Tony! there's the looking back. And, of all women, you!'

'Or else, dear-well, perhaps once on foreign soil, in a different air, I might—might have looked back, and seen my whole self, not shattered, as I feel it now, and come home again compassionate to the poor persecuted animal to defend her. Perhaps that was what I was running away for. I fled on the instinct, often a good thing to trust.'

'I saw you at The Crossways.'

'I remembered I had the dread that you would, though I did not imagine you would reach me so swiftly. My going there was an instinct, too. I suppose we are all instinct when we have the world at our heels. Forgive me if I generalize without any longer the right to be included in the common human sum. "Pariah" and "taboo" are words we borrow from barbarous tribes; they stick to me.'

'My Tony, you look as bright as ever, and you speak despairingly.'

'Call me enigma. I am that to myself, Emmy.'

'You are not quite yourself to your friend.'

'Since the blow I have been bewildered; I see nothing upright. It came on me suddenly; stunned me. A bolt out of a clear sky, as they say. He spared me a scene: There had been threats, and yet the sky was clear, or seemed. When we have a man for arbiter, he is our sky.'

Emma pressed her Tony's unresponsive hand, feeling strangely that her friend ebbed from her.

'Has he . . . to mislead him?' she said, colouring at the breach in the question.

'Proofs? He has the proofs he supposes.'

'Not to justify suspicion?'

'He broke open my desk and took my letters.'

'Horrible! But the letters?' Emma shook with a nervous revulsion.

'You might read them.'

'Basest of men! That is the unpardonable cowardice!', exclaimed Emma.

'The world will read them, dear,' said Diana, and struck herself to ice. She broke from the bitter frigidity in fury. 'They are letters—

none very long—sometimes two short sentences—he wrote at any spare moment. On my honour, as a woman, I feel for him most. The letters—I would bear any accusation rather than that exposure. Letters of a man of his age to a young woman he rates too highly!

The world reads them. Do you hear it saying it could have excused her for that fiddle-faddle with a younger—a young lover? And had I thought of a lover! . . . I had no thought of loving or being loved. I confess I was flattered. To you, Emma, I will confess . . . . You see the public ridicule!—and half his age, he and I would have appeared a romantic couple! Confess, I said. Well, dear, the stake is lighted for a trial of its effect on me. It is this: he was never a dishonourable friend; but men appear to be capable of friendship with women only for as long as we keep out of pulling distance of that line where friendship ceases. They may step on it; we must hold back a league. I have learnt it. You will judge whether he disrespects me. As for him, he is a man; at his worst, not one of the worst; at his best, better than very many. There, now, Emma, you have me stripped and burning; there is my full confession. Except for this—yes, one thing further—that I do rage at the ridicule, and could choose, but for you, to have given the world cause to revile me, or think me romantic. Something or somebody to suffer for would really be agreeable. It is a singular fact, I have not known what this love is, that they talk about. And behold me marched into Smithfield!—society's heretic, if you please. I must own I think it hard.'

Emma chafed her cold hand softly.

'It is hard; I understand it,' she murmured. 'And is your Sunday visit to us in the list of offences?'

'An item.'

'You gave me a happy day.'

'Then it counts for me in heaven.'

'He set spies on you?'

'So we may presume.'

Emma went through a sphere of tenuious reflections in a flash.

'He will rue it. Perhaps now . . . he may now be regretting his wretched frenzy. And Tony could pardon; she has the power of pardoning in her heart.'

'Oh! certainly, dear. But tell me why it is you speak to-night rather unlike the sedate, philosophical Emma; in a tone-well, tolerably sentimental?'

'I am unaware of it,' said Emma, who could have retorted with a like reproach. 'I am anxious, I will not say at present for your happiness, for your peace; and I have a hope that possibly a timely word from some friend—Lukin or another—might induce him to consider.'

'To pardon me, do you mean?' cried Diana, flushing sternly.

'Not pardon. Suppose a case of faults on both sides.'

'You address a faulty person, my dear. But do you know that you are hinting at a reconcilement?'

'Might it not be?'

'Open your eyes to what it involves. I trust I can pardon. Let him go his ways, do his darkest, or repent. But return to the roof of the "basest of men," who was guilty of "the unpardonable cowardice"? You expect me to be superhuman. When I consent to that, I shall be out of my woman's skin, which he has branded. Go back to him!' She was taken with a shudder of head and limbs. 'No; I really have the power of pardoning, and I am bound to; for among my debts to him, this present exemption, that is like liberty dragging a chain, or, say, an escaped felon wearing his manacles, should count. I am sensible of my obligation. The price I pay for it is an immovable patch-attractive to male idiots, I have heard, and a mark of scorn to females. Between the two the remainder of my days will be lively. "Out, out, damned spot!" But it will not. And not on the hand—on the forehead! We'll talk of it no longer. I have sent a note, with an enclosure, to my lawyers. I sell The Crossways, if I have the married woman's right to any scrap of property, for money to scatter fees.'

'My purse, dear Tony!' exclaimed Emma. 'My house! You will stay with me? Why do you shake your head? With me you are safe.' She spied at the shadows in her friend's face. 'Ever since your marriage, Tony, you have been strange in your trick of refusing to stay with me. And you and I made our friendship the pledge of a belief in eternity! We vowed it. Come, I do talk sentimentally, but my heart is in it. I beg you—all the reasons are with me—to make my house your home. You will. You know I am rather lonely.'

Diana struggled to keep her resolution from being broken by tenderness. And doubtless poor Sir Lukin had learnt his lesson; still, her defensive instincts could never quite slumber under his roof; not because of any further fear that they would have to be summoned; it was chiefly owing to the consequences of his treacherous foolishness. For this half-home with her friend thenceforward denied to her, she had accepted a protector, called husband—rashly, past credence, in the retrospect; but it had been her propelling motive; and the loathings roused by her marriage helped to sicken her at the idea of a lengthened stay where she had suffered the shock precipitating her to an act of insanity.

'I do not forget you were an heiress, Emmy, and I will come to you if I need money to keep my head up. As for staying, two reasons are against it. If I am to fight my battle, I must be seen; I must go about— wherever I am received. So my field is London. That is obvious. And I shall rest better in a house where my story is not known.'

Two or three questions ensued. Diana had to fortify her fictitious objection by alluding to her maid's prattle of the household below; and she excused the hapless, overfed, idle people of those regions.

To Emma it seemed a not unnatural sensitiveness. She came to a settled resolve in her thoughts, as she said, 'They want a change. London is their element.'

Feeling that she deceived this true heart, however lightly and necessarily, Diana warmed to her, forgiving her at last for having netted and dragged her back to front the enemy; an imposition of horrors, of which the scene and the travelling with Redworth, the talking of her case with her most intimate friend as well, had been a distempering foretaste.

They stood up and kissed, parting for the night.

An odd world, where for the sin we have not participated in we must fib and continue fibbing, she reflected. She did not entirely cheat her clearer mind, for she perceived that her step in flight had been urged both by a weak despondency and a blind desperation; also that the world of a fluid civilization is perforce artificial. But her mind was in the background of her fevered senses, and when she looked in the glass and mused on uttering the word, 'Liar!' to the lovely image, her senses were refreshed, her mind somewhat relieved, the face appeared so sovereignly defiant of abasement.

Thus did a nature distraught by pain obtain some short lull of repose. Thus, moreover, by closely reading herself, whom she scourged to excess that she might in justice be comforted, she gathered an increasing knowledge of our human constitution, and stored matter for the brain.

CHAPTER XIII.
TOUCHING THE FIRST DAYS OF HER PROBATION

The result of her sleeping was, that Diana's humour, locked up overnight, insisted on an excursion, as she lay with half-buried head and open eyelids, thinking of the firm of lawyers she had to see; and to whom, and to the legal profession generally, she would be, under outward courtesies, nothing other than 'the woman Warwick.' She pursued the woman Warwick unmercifully through a series of interviews with her decorous and crudely-minded defenders; accurately perusing them behind their senior staidness. Her scorching sensitiveness sharpened her intelligence in regard to the estimate of discarded wives entertained by men of business and plain men of the world, and she drove the woman Warwick down their ranks, amazed by the vision of a puppet so unlike to herself in reality, though identical in situation. That woman, reciting her side of the case, gained a gradual resemblance to Danvers; she spoke primly; perpetually the creature aired her handkerchief; she was bent on softening those sugarloaves, the hard business-men applying to her for facts. Facts were treated as unworthy of her; mere stuff of the dustheap, mutton-bones, old shoes; she swam above them in a cocoon of her spinning, sylphidine, unseizable; and between perplexing and mollifying the slaves of facts, she saw them at their heels, a tearful fry, abjectly imitative of her melodramatic performances. The spectacle was presented of a band of legal gentlemen vociferating mightily for swords and the onset, like the Austrian empress's Magyars, to vindicate her just and holy cause. Our Law-courts failing, they threatened Parliament, and for a last resort, the country! We are not going to be the woman Warwick without a stir, my brethren.

Emma, an early riser that morning, for the purpose of a private consultation with Mr. Redworth, found her lying placidly wakeful, to judge by appearances.

'You have not slept, my dear child?'

'Perfectly,' said Diana, giving her hand and offering the lips. 'I'm only having a warm morning bath in bed,' she added, in explanation of a chill moisture that the touch of her exposed skin betrayed; for whatever the fun of the woman Warwick, there had been sympathetic feminine horrors in the frame of the sentient woman.

Emma fancied she kissed a quiet sufferer. A few remarks very soon set her wildly laughing. Both were laughing when Danvers entered the room, rather guilty, being late; and the sight of the prim-visaged maid she had been driving among the lawyers kindled Diana's comic imagination to such a pitch that she ran riot in drolleries, carrying her friend headlong on the tide.

'I have not laughed so much since you were married,' said Emma.

'Nor I, dear; proving that the bar to it was the ceremony,' said Diana.

She promised to remain at Copsley three days. 'Then for the campaign in Mr. Redworth's metropolis. I wonder whether I may ask him to get me lodgings: a sitting-room and two bedrooms. The Crossways has a board up for letting. I should prefer to be my own tenant; only it would give me a hundred pounds more to get a substitute's money. I should like to be at work writing instantly. Ink is my opium, and the pen my nigger, and he must dig up gold for me. It is written. Danvers, you can make ready to dress me when I ring.'

Emma helped the beautiful woman to her dressing-gown and the step from her bed. She had her thoughts, and went down to Redworth at the breakfast-table, marvelling that any husband other than a madman could cast such a jewel away. The material loveliness eclipses intellectual qualities in such reflections.

'He must be mad,' she said, compelled to disburden herself in a congenial atmosphere; which, however, she infrigidated by her overflow of exclamatory wonderment—a curtain that shook voluminous folds, luring Redworth to dreams of the treasure forfeited. He became rigidly practical.

'Provision will have to be made for her. Lukin must see Mr. Warwick. She will do wisely to stay with friends in town, mix in company. Women are the best allies for such cases. Who are her solicitors?'

'They are mine: Braddock, Thorpe, and Simnel.'

'A good firm. She is in safe hands with them. I dare say they may come to an arrangement.'

'I should wish it. She will never consent.'

Redworth shrugged. A woman's 'never' fell far short of outstripping the sturdy pedestrian Time, to his mind.

Diana saw him drive off to catch the coach in the valley, regulated to meet the train, and much though she liked him, she was not sorry that he had gone. She felt the better clad for it. She would have rejoiced to witness the departure on wings of all her friends, except Emma, to whom her coldness overnight had bound her anew warmly in contrition. And yet her friends were well-beloved by her; but her emotions were distraught.

Emma told her that Mr. Redworth had undertaken to hire a suite of convenient rooms, and to these she looked forward, the nest among strangers, where she could begin to write, earning bread: an idea that, with the pride of independence, conjured the pleasant morning smell of a bakery about her.

She passed three peaceable days at Copsley, at war only with the luxury of the house. On the fourth, a letter to Lady Dunstane from Redworth gave the address of the best lodgings he could find, and Diana started for London.

She had during a couple of weeks, besides the first fresh exercising of her pen, as well as the severe gratification of economy, a savage exultation in passing through the streets on foot and unknown. Save for the plunges into the office of her solicitors, she could seem to herself a woman who had never submitted to the yoke. What a pleasure it was, after finishing a number of pages, to start Eastward toward the lawyer- regions, full of imaginary cropping incidents, and from that churchyard Westward, against smoky sunsets, or in welcome fogs, an atom of the crowd! She had an affection for the crowd. They clothed her. She laughed at the gloomy forebodings of Danvers concerning the perils environing ladies in the streets after dark alone. The lights in the streets after dark and the quick running of her blood, combined to strike sparks of fancy and inspirit the task of composition at night. This new, strange, solitary life, cut off from her adulatory society, both by the shock that made the abyss and by the utter foreignness, threw her in upon her natural forces, recasting her, and thinning away her memory of her past days, excepting girlhood, into the remote. She lived with her girlhood as with a simple little sister. They were two in one, and she corrected the dreams of the younger, protected and counselled her very sagely, advising her to love Truth and look always to Reality for her refreshment. She was ready to say, that no habitable spot on our planet was healthier and pleasanter than London. As to the perils haunting the head of Danvers, her experiences assured her of a perfect immunity from them; and the maligned thoroughfares of a great city, she was ready to affirm, contrasted favourably with certain hospitable halls.

The long-suffering Fates permitted her for a term to enjoy the generous delusion. Subsequently a sweet surprise alleviated the shock she had sustained. Emma Dunstane's carriage was at her door, and Emma entered her sitting-room, to tell her of having hired a house in the neighbourhood, looking on the park. She begged to have her for guest, sorrowfully anticipating the refusal. At least they were to be near one another.

'You really like this life in lodgings?' asked Emma, to whom the stiff furniture and narrow apartments were a dreariness, the miserably small fire of the sitting-room an aspect of cheerless winter.

'I do,' said Diana; 'yes,' she added with some reserve, and smiled at her damped enthusiasm, 'I can eat when I like, walk, work—and I am working! My legs and my pen demand it. Let me be independent! Besides, I begin to learn something of the bigger world outside the one I know, and I crush my mincing tastes. In return for that, I get a sense of strength I had not when I was a drawing-room exotic. Much is repulsive. But I am taken with a passion for reality.'

They spoke of the lawyers, and the calculated period of the trial; of the husband too, in his inciting belief in the falseness of his wife. 'That is his excuse,' Diana said, her closed mouth meditatively dimpling the comers over thoughts of his grounds for fury. He had them, though none for the incriminating charge. The Sphinx mouth of the married woman at war and at bay must be left unriddled. She and the law differed in their interpretation of the dues of wedlock.

But matters referring to her case were secondary with Diana beside the importance of her storing impressions. Her mind required to hunger for something, and this Reality which frequently she was forced to loathe, she forced herself proudly to accept, despite her youthfulness. Her philosophy swallowed it in the lump, as the great serpent his meal; she hoped to digest it sleeping likewise. Her visits of curiosity to the Law Courts, where she stood spying and listening behind a veil, gave her a great deal of tough substance to digest. There she watched the process of the tortures to be applied to herself, and hardened her senses for the ordeal. She saw there the ribbed and shanked old skeleton world on which our fair fleshly is moulded. After all, your Fool's Paradise is not a garden to grow in. Charon's ferry-boat is not thicker with phantoms. They do not live in mind or soul. Chiefly women people it: a certain class of limp men; women for the most part: they are sown there. And put their garden under the magnifying glass of intimacy, what do we behold? A world not better than the world it curtains, only foolisher.

Her conversations with Lady Dunstane brought her at last to the point of her damped enthusiasm. She related an incident or two occurring in her career of independence, and they discussed our state of civilization plainly and gravely, save for the laughing peals her phrases occasionally provoked; as when she named the intruders and disturbers of solitarily- faring ladies, 'Cupid's footpads.' Her humour was created to swim on waters where a prescribed and cultivated prudery should pretend to be drowning.

'I was getting an exalted idea of English gentlemen, Emmy. "Rich and rare were the gems she wore." I was ready to vow that one might traverse the larger island similarly respected. I praised their chivalry. I thought it a privilege to live in such a land. I cannot describe to you how delightful it was to me to walk out and home generally protected. I might have been seriously annoyed but that one of the clerks- "articled," he called himself—of our lawyers happened to be by. He offered to guard me, and was amusing with his modest tiptoe air. No, I trust to the English common man more than ever. He is a man of honour. I am convinced he is matchless in any other country, except Ireland. The English gentleman trades on his reputation.'

He was condemned by an afflicted delicacy, the sharpest of critical tribunals.

Emma bade her not to be too sweeping from a bad example.

'It is not a single one,' said Diana. 'What vexes me and frets me is, that I must be a prisoner, or allow Danvers to mount guard. And I can't see the end of it. And Danvers is no magician. She seems to know her countrymen, though. She warded one of them off, by saying to me: "This is the crossing, my lady." He fled.'

Lady Dunstane affixed the popular title to the latter kind of gentleman. She was irritated on her friend's behalf, and against the worrying of her sisterhood, thinking in her heart, nevertheless, that the passing of a face and figure like Diana's might inspire honourable emotions, pitiable for being hapless.

'If you were with me, dear, you would have none of these annoyances,' she said, pleading forlornly.

Diana smiled to herself. 'No! I should relapse into softness. This life exactly suits my present temper. My landlady is respectful and attentive; the little housemaid is a willing slave; Danvers does not despise them pugnaciously; they make a home for me, and I am learning daily. Do you know, the less ignorant I become, the more considerate I am for the ignorance of others—I love them for it.' She squeezed Emma's hand with more meaning than her friend apprehended. 'So I win my advantage from the trifles I have to endure. They are really trifles, and I should once have thought them mountains!'

For the moment Diana stipulated that she might not have to encounter friends or others at Lady Dunstane's dinner-table, and the season not being favourable to those gatherings planned by Lady Dunstane in her project of winning supporters, there was a respite, during which Sir Lukin worked manfully at his three Clubs to vindicate Diana's name from the hummers and hawers, gaining half a dozen hot adherents, and a body of lukewarm, sufficiently stirred to be desirous to see the lady. He worked with true champion zeal, although an interview granted him by the husband settled his opinion as to any possibility of the two ever coming to terms. Also it struck him that if he by misadventure had been a woman and the wife of such a fellow, by Jove! . . .his apostrophe to the father of the gods of pagandom signifying the amount of matter Warwick would have had reason to complain of in earnest. By ricochet his military mind rebounded from his knowledge of himself to an ardent, faith in Mrs. Warwick's innocence; for, as there was no resemblance between them, there must, he deduced, be a difference in their capacity for enduring the perpetual company of a prig, a stick, a petrified poser. Moreover, the novel act of advocacy, and the nature of the advocacy, had effect on him. And then he recalled the scene in the winter beech-woods, and Diana's wild-deer eyes; her, perfect generosity to a traitor and fool. How could he have doubted her? Glimpses of the corrupting cause for it partly penetrated his density: a conqueror of ladies, in mid- career, doubts them all. Of course he had meant no harm, nothing worse than some petty philandering with the loveliest woman of her time. And, by Jove! it was worth the rebuff to behold the Beauty in her wrath.

The reflections of Lothario, however much tending tardily to do justice to a particular lady, cannot terminate wholesomely. But he became a gallant partisan. His portrayal of Mr. Warwick to his wife and his friends was fine caricature. 'The fellow had his hand up at my first word—stood like a sentinel under inspection. "Understand, Sir Lukin, that I receive you simply as an acquaintance. As an intermediary, permit me to state that you are taking superfluous trouble. The case must proceed. It is final. She is at liberty, in the meantime, to draw on my bankers for the provision she may need, at the rate of five hundred pounds per annum." He spoke of "the lady now bearing my name." He was within an inch of saying "dishonouring." I swear I heard the "dis," and he caught himself up. He "again declined any attempt towards reconciliation." It could "only be founded on evasion of the truth to be made patent on the day of trial." Half his talk was lawyers' lingo. The fellow's teeth looked like frost. If Lot's wife had a brother, his name's Warwick. How Diana Merion, who could have had the pick of the best of us, ever came to marry a fellow like that, passes my comprehension, queer creatures as women are! He can ride; that's about all he can do. I told him Mrs. Warwick had no thought of reconciliation. "Then, Sir Lukin, you will perceive that we have no standpoint for a discussion." I told him the point was, for a man of honour not to drag his wife before the public, as he had no case to stand on—less than nothing. You should have seen the fellow's face. He shot a sneer up to his eyelids, and flung his head back. So I said, "Good-day." He marches me to the door, "with his compliments to Lady Dunstane." I could have floored him for that. Bless my soul, what fellows the world is made of, when here's a man, calling himself a gentleman, who, just because he gets in a rage with his wife for one thing or another—and past all competition the handsomest woman of her day, and the cleverest, the nicest, the best of the whole boiling— has her out for a public horsewhipping, and sets all the idiots of the kingdom against her! I tried to reason with him. He made as if he were going to sleep standing.'

Sir Lukin gratified Lady Dunstane by his honest championship of Diana. And now, in his altered mood (the thrice indebted rogue was just cloudily conscious of a desire to propitiate his dear wife by serving her friend), he began a crusade against the scandal-newspapers, going with an Irish military comrade straight to the editorial offices, and leaving his card and a warning that the chastisement for print of the name of the lady in their columns would be personal and condign. Captain Carew Mahony, albeit unacquainted with Mrs. Warwick, had espoused her cause. She was a woman, she was an Irishwoman, she was a beautiful woman. She had, therefore, three positive claims on him as a soldier and a man. Other Irish gentlemen, animated by the same swelling degrees, were awaking to the intimation that they might be wanted. Some words were dropped here and there by General Lord Larrian: he regretted his age and infirmities. A goodly regiment for a bodyguard might have been selected to protect her steps in the public streets; when it was bruited that the General had sent her a present of his great Newfoundland dog, Leander, to attend on her and impose a required respect. But as it chanced that her address was unknown to the volunteer constabulary, they had to assuage their ardour by thinking the dog luckier than they.

The report of the dog was a fact. He arrived one morning at Diana's lodgings, with a soldier to lead him, and a card to introduce:— the Hercules of dogs, a very ideal of the species, toweringly big, benevolent, reputed a rescuer of lives, disdainful of dog-fighting, devoted to his guardian's office, with a majestic paw to give and the noblest satisfaction in receiving caresses ever expressed by mortal male enfolded about the head, kissed, patted, hugged, snuggled, informed that he was his new mistress's one love and darling.

She despatched a thrilling note of thanks to Lord Larrian, sure of her touch upon an Irish heart.

The dog Leander soon responded to the attachment of a mistress enamoured of him. 'He is my husband,' she said to Emma, and started a tear in the eyes of her smiling friend; 'he promises to trust me, and never to have the law of me, and to love my friends as his own; so we are certain to agree.' In rain, snow, sunshine, through the parks and the streets, he was the shadow of Diana, commanding, on the whole, apart from some desperate attempts to make him serve as introducer, a civilized behaviour in the legions of Cupid's footpads. But he helped, innocently enough, to create an enemy.

CHAPTER XIV.
GIVING GLIMPSES OF DIANA UNDER HER CLOUD BEFORE THE WORLD AND OF HER FURTHER APPRENTICESHIP

As the day of her trial became more closely calculable, Diana's anticipated alarms receded with the deadening of her heart to meet the shock. She fancied she had put on proof-armour, unconscious that it was the turning of the inward flutterer to steel, which supplied her cuirass and shield. The necessity to brave society, in the character of honest Defendant, caused but a momentary twitch of the nerves. Her heart beat regularly, like a serviceable clock; none of her faculties abandoned her save songfulness, and none belied her, excepting a disposition to tartness almost venomous in the sarcastic shafts she let fly at friends interceding with Mr. Warwick to spare his wife, when she had determined to be tried. A strange fit of childishness overcame her powers of thinking, and was betrayed in her manner of speaking, though—to herself her dwindled humour allowed her to appear the towering Britomart. She pouted contemptuously on hearing that a Mr. Sullivan Smith (a remotely recollected figure) had besought Mr. Warwick for an interview, and gained it, by stratagem, 'to bring the man to his senses': but an ultra-Irishman did not compromise her battle-front, as the busybody supplications of a personal friend like Mr. Redworth did; and that the latter, without consulting her, should be 'one of the plaintive crew whining about the heels of the Plaintiff for a mercy she disdained and rejected' was bitter to her taste.

'He does not see that unless I go through the fire there is no justification for this wretched character of mine!' she exclaimed. Truce, treaty, withdrawal, signified publicly pardon, not exoneration by any means; and now that she was in armour she had no dread of the public. So she said. Redworth's being then engaged upon the canvass of a borough, added to the absurdity of his meddling with the dilemmas of a woman. 'Dear me, Emma! think of stepping aside from the parliamentary road to entreat a husband to relent, and arrange the domestic alliance of a contrary couple! Quixottry is agreeable reading, a silly performance.' Lady Dunstane pleaded his friendship. She had to quit the field where such darts were showering.

The first dinner-party was aristocratic, easy to encounter. Lord and Lady Crane, Lady Pennon, Lord and Lady Esquart, Lord Larrian, Mr. and Mrs. Montvert of Halford Manor, Lady Singleby, Sir Walter Capperston friends, admirers of Diana; patrons, in the phrase of the time, of her father, were the guests. Lady Pennon expected to be amused, and was gratified, for Diana had only to open her mouth to set the great lady laughing. She petitioned to have Mrs. Warwick at her table that day week, because the marquis was dying to make her acquaintance, and begged to have all her sayings repeated to him; vowed she must be salt in the desert. 'And remember, I back you through thick and thin,' said Lady Pennon. To which Diana replied: 'If I am salt in the desert, you are the spring'; and the old lady protested she must put that down for her book. The witty Mrs. Warwick, of whom wit was expected, had many incitements to be guilty of cheap wit; and the beautiful Mrs. Warwick, being able to pass anything she uttered, gave good and bad alike, under the impulsion to give out something, that the stripped and shivering Mrs. Warwick might find a cover in applause. She discovered the social uses of cheap wit; she laid ambushes for anecdotes, a telling form of it among a people of no conversational interlocution, especially in the circles depending for dialogue upon perpetual fresh supplies of scandal; which have plentiful crops, yet not sufficient. The old dinner and supper tables at The Crossways furnished her with an abundant store; and recollection failing, she invented. Irish anecdotes are always popular in England, as promoting, besides the wholesome shake of the sides, a kindly sense of superiority. Anecdotes also are portable, unlike the lightning flash, which will not go into the pocket; they can be carried home, they are disbursable at other tables. These were Diana's weapons. She was perforce the actress of her part.

In happier times, when light of heart and natural, her vogue had not been so enrapturing. Doubtless Cleopatra in her simple Egyptian uniform would hardly have won such plaudits as her stress of barbaric Oriental splendours evoked for her on the swan and serpent

Nile-barge—not from posterity at least. It is a terrible decree, that all must act who would prevail; and the more extended the audience, the greater need for the mask and buskin.

From Lady Pennon's table Diana passed to Lady Crane's, Lady Esquart's, Lady Singleby's, the Duchess of Raby's, warmly clad in the admiration she excited. She appeared at Princess Therese Paryli's first ball of the season, and had her circle, not of worshippers only. She did not dance. The princess, a fair Austrian, benevolent to her sisterhood, an admirer of Diana's contrasting complexion, would have had her dance once in a quadrille of her forming, but yielded to the mute expression of the refusal. Wherever Mrs. Warwick went, her arts of charming were addressed to the women. Men may be counted on for falling bowled over by a handsome face and pointed tongue; women require some wooing from their ensphered and charioted sister, particularly if she is clouded; and old women—excellent buttresses— must be suavely courted. Now, to woo the swimming matron and court the settled dowager, she had to win forgiveness for her beauty; and this was done, easily done, by forbearing to angle with it in the press of nibblers. They ranged about her, individually unnoticed. Seeming unaware of its effect where it kindled, she smote a number of musical female chords, compassion among them. A general grave affability of her eyes and smiles was taken for quiet pleasure in the scene. Her fitful intentness of look when conversing with the older ladies told of the mind within at work upon what they said, and she was careful that plain dialogue should make her comprehensible to them. Nature taught her these arts, through which her wit became extolled entirely on the strength of her reputation, and her beauty did her service by never taking aim abroad. They are the woman's arts of self- defence, as legitimately and honourably hers as the manful use of the fists with a coarser sex. If it had not been nature that taught her the practice of them in extremity, the sagacious dowagers would have seen brazenness rather than innocence—or an excuseable indiscretion—in the part she was performing. They are not lightly duped by one of their sex. Few tasks are more difficult than for a young woman under a cloud to hoodwink old women of the world. They are the prey of financiers, but Time has presented them a magic ancient glass to scan their sex in.

At Princess Paryli's Ball two young men of singular elegance were observed by Diana, little though she concentered her attention on any figures of the groups. She had the woman's faculty (transiently bestowed by perfervid jealousy upon men) of distinguishing minutely in the calmest of indifferent glances. She could see without looking; and when her eyes were wide they had not to dwell to be detective. It did not escape her that the Englishman of the two hurried for the chance of an introduction, nor that he suddenly, after putting a question to a man beside him, retired. She spoke of them to Emma as they drove home. 'The princess's partner in the first quadrille . . . Hungarian, I suppose? He was like a Tartar modelled by a Greek: supple as the Scythian's bow, braced as the string! He has the air of a born horseman, and valses perfectly. I won't say he was handsomer than a young Englishman there, but he had the advantage of soldierly training. How different is that quick springy figure from our young men's lounging style! It comes of military exercise and discipline.'

'That was Count Jochany, a cousin of the princess, and a cavalry officer,' said Emma. 'You don't know the other? I am sure the one you mean must be Percy Dacier.'

His retiring was explained: the Hon. Percy Dacier was the nephew of Lord Dannisburgh, often extolled to her as the promising youngster of his day, with the reserve that he wasted his youth: for the young gentleman was decorous and studious; ambitious, according to report; a politician taking to politics much too seriously and exclusively to suit his uncle's pattern for the early period of life. Uncle and nephew went their separate ways, rarely meeting, though their exchange of esteem was cordial.

Thinking over his abrupt retirement from the crowded semicircle, Diana felt her position pinch her, she knew not why.

Lady Dunstane was as indefatigable by day as by night in the business of acting goddess to her beloved Tony, whom she assured that the service, instead of exhausting, gave her such healthfulness as she had imagined herself to have lost for ever. The word was passed, and invitations poured in to choice conversational breakfasts, private afternoon concerts, all the humming season's assemblies. Mr. Warwick's treatment of his wife was taken by implication for lunatic; wherever she was heard or seen, he had no case; a jury of some hundreds of both sexes, ready to be sworn, pronounced against him.

Only the personal enemies of the lord in the suit presumed to doubt, and they exercised the discretion of a minority.

But there is an upper middle class below the aristocratic, boasting an aristocracy of morals, and eminently persuasive of public opinion, if not commanding it. Previous to the relaxation, by amendment, of a certain legal process, this class was held to represent the austerity of the country. At present a relaxed austerity is represented; and still the bulk of the members are of fair repute, though not quite on the level of their pretensions. They were then, while more sharply divided from the titular superiors they are socially absorbing, very powerful to brand a woman's character, whatever her rank might be; having innumerable agencies and avenues for that high purpose, to say nothing of the printing-press. Lady Dunstane's anxiety to draw them over to the cause of her friend set her thinking of the influential Mrs. Cramborne Wathin, with whom she was distantly connected; the wife of a potent serjeant-at- law fast mounting to the Bench and knighthood; the centre of a circle, and not strangely that, despite her deficiency in the arts and graces, for she had wealth and a cook, a husband proud of his wine-cellar, and the ambition to rule; all the rewards, together with the expectations, of the virtuous. She was a lady of incisive features bound in stale parchment. Complexion she had none, but she had spotlessness of skin, and sons and daughters just resembling her, like cheaper editions of a precious quarto of a perished type. You discerned the imitation of the type, you acknowledged the inferior compositor. Mr. Cramborne Wathin was by birth of a grade beneath his wife; he sprang (behind a curtain of horror) from tradesmen. The Bench was in designation for him to wash out the stain, but his children suffered in large hands and feet, short legs, excess of bone, prominences misplaced. Their mother inspired them carefully with the religion she opposed to the pretensions of a nobler blood, while instilling into them that the blood they drew from her was territorial, far above the vulgar. Her appearance and her principles fitted her to stand for the Puritan rich of the period, emerging by the aid of an extending wealth into luxurious worldliness, and retaining the maxims of their forefathers for the discipline of the poor and erring.

Lady Dunstane called on her, ostensibly to let her know she had taken a house in town for the season, and in the course of the chat Mrs.

Cramborne Wathin was invited to dinner. 'You will meet my dear friend, Mrs. Warwick,' she said, and the reply was: 'Oh, I have heard of her.'

The formal consultation with Mr. Cramborne Wathin ended in an agreement to accept Lady Dunstane's kind invitation.

Considering her husband's plenitude of old legal anecdotes, and her own diligent perusal of the funny publications of the day, that she might be on the level of the wits and celebrities she entertained, Mrs. Cramborne Wathin had a right to expect the leading share in the conversation to which she was accustomed. Every honour was paid to them; they met aristocracy in the persons of Lord Larrian, of Lady Rockden, Colonel Purlby, the Pettigrews, but neither of them held the table for a moment; the topics flew, and were no sooner up than down; they were unable to get a shot. They had to eat in silence, occasionally grinning, because a woman labouring under a stigma would rattle-rattle, as if the laughter of the company were her due, and decency beneath her notice. Some one alluded to a dog of Mrs. Warwick's, whereupon she trips out a story of her dog's amazing intelligence.

'And pray,' said Mrs. Cramborne Wathin across the table, merely to slip in a word, 'what is the name of this wonderful dog?'

'His name is Leander,' said Diana.

'Oh, Leander. I don't think I hear myself calling to a dog in a name of three syllables. Two at the most.'

No, so I call Hero! if I want him to come immediately,' said Diana, and the gentlemen, to Mrs. Cramborne Wathin's astonishment, acclaimed it. Mr. Redworth, at her elbow, explained the point, to her disgust. . .

That was Diana's offence.

If it should seem a small one, let it be remembered that a snub was intended, and was foiled; and foiled with an apparent simplicity, enough to exasperate, had there been no laughter of men to back the countering stroke. A woman under a cloud, she talked, pushed to shine; she would be heard, would be applauded. Her chronicler must likewise admit the error of her giving way to a petty sentiment of antagonism on first beholding Mrs. Cramborne Wathin, before whom she at once resolved to be herself, for a holiday, instead of acting demurely to conciliate. Probably it was an antagonism of race, the shrinking of the skin from the burr. But when Tremendous Powers are invoked, we should treat any simple revulsion of our blood as a vice. The Gods of this world's contests demand it of us, in relation to them, that the mind, and not the instincts, shall be at work. Otherwise the course of a prudent policy is never to invoke them, but avoid.

The upper class was gained by her intrepidity, her charm, and her elsewhere offending wit, however the case might go. It is chivalrous, but not, alas, inflammable in support of innocence. The class below it is governed in estimates of character by accepted patterns of conduct; yet where innocence under persecution is believed to exist, the members animated by that belief can be enthusiastic. Enthusiasm is a heaven-sent steeplechaser, and takes a flying leap of the ordinary barriers; it is more intrusive than chivalry, and has a passion to communicate its ardour. Two letters from stranger ladies reached Diana, through her lawyers and Lady Dunstane. Anonymous letters, not so welcome, being male effusions, arrived at her lodgings, one of them comical almost over the verge to pathos in its termination: 'To me you will ever be the Goddess Diana—my faith in woman!'

He was unacquainted with her!

She had not the heart to think the writers donkeys. How they obtained her address was a puzzle; they stole in to comfort her slightly. They attached her to her position of Defendant by the thought of what would have been the idea of her character if she had flown—a reflection emanating from inexperience of the resources of sentimentalists.

If she had flown! She was borne along by the tide like a butterfly that a fish may gobble unless a friendly hand shall intervene. And could it in nature? She was past expectation of release. The attempt to imagine living with any warmth of blood in her vindicated character, for the sake of zealous friends, consigned her to a cold and empty house upon a foreign earth. She had to set her mind upon the mysterious enshrouded Twelve, with whom the verdict would soon be hanging, that she might prompt her human combativeness to desire the vindication at such a price as she would have to pay for it. When Emma Dunstane spoke to her of the certainty of triumphing, she suggested a possible dissentient among the fateful Twelve, merely to escape the drumming sound of that hollow big word. The irreverent imp of her humour came to her relief by calling forth the Twelve, in the tone of the clerk of the Court, and they answered to their names of trades and crafts after the manner of Titania's elves, and were questioned as to their fitness, by education, habits, enlightenment, to pronounce decisively upon the case in dispute, the case being plainly stated. They replied, that the long habit of dealing with scales enabled them to weigh the value of evidence the most delicate. Moreover, they were Englishmen, and anything short of downright bullet facts went to favour the woman. For thus we light the balance of legal injustice toward the sex: we conveniently wink, ma'am. A rough, old-fashioned way for us! Is it a Breach of Promise?—She may reckon on her damages: we have daughters of our own. Is it a suit for Divorce?—Well, we have wives of our own, and we can lash, or we can spare; that's as it may be; but we'll keep the couple tied, let 'em hate as they like, if they can't furnish pork-butchers' reasons for sundering; because the man makes the money in this country.—My goodness! what a funny people, sir!—It 's our way of holding the balance, ma'am.—But would it not be better to rectify the law and the social system, dear sir?—Why, ma'am, we find it comfortabler to take cases as they come, in the style of our fathers.—But don't you see, my good man, that you are offering scapegoats for the comfort of the majority?—Well, ma'am, there always were scapegoats, and always will be; we find it comes round pretty square in the end.

'And I may be the scapegoat, Emmy! It is perfectly possible. The grocer, the pork-butcher, drysalter, stationer, tea-merchant, et caetera —they sit on me. I have studied the faces of the juries, and Mr. Braddock tells me of their composition. And he admits that they do justice roughly—a rough and tumble country! to quote him—though he says they are honest in intention.'

'More shame to the man who drags you before them—if he persists!' Emma rejoined.

'He will. I know him. I would not have him draw back now,' said Diana, catching her breath. 'And, dearest, do not abuse him; for if you do, you set me imagining guiltiness. Oh, heaven!—suppose me publicly pardoned! No, I have kinder feelings when we stand opposed. It is odd, and rather frets my conscience, to think of the little resentment I feel. Hardly any! He has not cause to like his wife. I can own it, and I am sorry for him, heartily. No two have ever come together so naturally antagonistic as we two. We walked a dozen steps in stupefied union, and hit upon crossways. From that moment it was tug and tug; he me, I him. By resisting, I made him a tyrant; and he, by insisting, made me a rebel. And he was the maddest of tyrants—a weak one. My dear, he was also a double-dealer. Or no, perhaps not in design. He was moved at one time by his interests; at another by his idea of his honour. He took what I could get for him, and then turned and drubbed me for getting it.'

'This is the creature you try to excuse!' exclaimed indignant Emma.

'Yes, because—but fancy all the smart things I said being called my "sallies"!—can a woman live with it?—because I behaved . . . I despised him too much, and I showed it. He is not a contemptible man before the world; he is merely a very narrow one under close inspection. I could not—or did not—conceal my feeling. I showed it not only to him, to my friend. Husband grew to mean to me stifler, lung-contractor, iron mask, inquisitor, everything anti-natural. He suffered under my "sallies": and it was the worse for him when he did not perceive their drift. He is an upright man; I have not seen marked meanness. One might build up a respectable figure in negatives. I could add a row of noughts to the single number he cherishes, enough to make a millionnaire of him; but strike away the first, the rest are wind. Which signifies, that if you do not take his estimate of himself, you will think little of his: negative virtues. He is not eminently, that is to say, not saliently, selfish; not rancorous, not obtrusive—tata-ta-ta. But dull!—dull as a woollen nightcap over eyes and ears and mouth. Oh! an executioner's black cap to me. Dull, and suddenly staring awake to the idea of his honour. I "rendered" him ridiculous—I had caught a trick of "using men's phrases." Dearest, now that the day of trial draws nigh—you have never questioned me, and it was like you to spare me pain—but now I can speak of him and myself.' Diana dropped her voice. Here was another confession. The proximity of the trial acted like fire on her faded recollection of incidents. It may be that partly the shame of alluding to them had blocked her woman's memory. For one curious operation of the charge of guiltiness upon the nearly guiltless is to make them paint themselves pure white, to the obliteration of minor spots, until the whiteness being acknowledged, or the ordeal imminent, the spots recur and press upon their consciences. She resumed, in a rapid undertone: 'You know that a certain degree of independence had been, if not granted by him, conquered by me. I had the habit of it. Obedience with him is imprisonment—he is a blind wall. He received a commission, greatly to his advantage, and was absent. He seems to have received information of some sort. He returned unexpectedly, at a late hour, and attacked me at once, middling violent. My friend—and that he is! was coming from the House for a ten minutes' talk, as usual, on his way home, to refresh him after the long sitting and bear-baiting he had nightly to endure. Now let me confess: I grew frightened; Mr. Warwick was "off his head," as they say-crazy, and I could not bear the thought of those two meeting. While he raged I threw open the window and put the lamp near it, to expose the whole interior—cunning as a veteran intriguer: horrible, but it had to be done to keep them apart. He asked me what madness possessed me, to sit by an open window at midnight, in view of the public, with a damp wind blowing. I complained of want of air and fanned my forehead. I heard the steps on the pavement; I stung him to retort loudly, and I was relieved; the steps passed on. So the trick succeeded—the trick! It was the worst I was guilty of, but it was a trick, and it branded me trickster. It teaches me to see myself with an abyss in my nature full of infernal possibilities. I think I am hewn in black rock. A woman who can do as I did by instinct, needs to have an angel always near her, if she has not a husband she reveres.'

'We are none of us better than you, dear Tony; only some are more fortunate, and many are cowards,' Emma said. 'You acted prudently in a wretched situation, partly of your own making, partly of the circumstances. But a nature like yours could not sit still and moan. That marriage was to blame! The English notion of women seems to be that we are born white sheep or black; circumstances have nothing to do with our colour. They dread to grant distinctions, and to judge of us discerningly is beyond them. Whether the fiction, that their homes are purer than elsewhere, helps to establish the fact, I do not know: there is a class that does live honestly; and at any rate it springs from a liking for purity; but I am sure that their method of impressing it on women has the dangers of things artificial. They narrow their understanding of human nature, and that is not the way to improve the breed.'

'I suppose we women are taken to be the second thoughts of the Creator; human nature's fringes, mere finishing touches, not a part of the texture,' said Diana; 'the pretty ornamentation. However, I fancy I perceive some tolerance growing in the minds of the dominant sex. Our old lawyer Mr. Braddock, who appears to have no distaste for conversations with me, assures me he expects the day to come when women will be encouraged to work at crafts and professions for their independence. That is the secret of the opinion of us at present— our dependency. Give us the means of independence, and we will gain it, and have a turn at judging you, my lords! You shall behold a world reversed. Whenever I am distracted by existing circumstances, I lay my finger on the material conditions, and I touch the secret. Individually, it may be moral with us; collectively, it is material-gross wrongs, gross hungers. I am a married rebel, and thereof comes the social rebel. I was once a dancing and singing girl: You remember the night of the Dublin Ball. A Channel sea in uproar, stirred by witches, flows between.'

'You are as lovely as you were then—I could say, lovelier,' said Emma.

'I have unconquerable health, and I wish I could give you the half of it, dear. I work late into the night, and I wake early and fresh in the morning. I do not sing, that is all. A few days more, and my character will be up before the Bull's Head to face him in the arena. The worst of a position like mine is, that it causes me incessantly to think and talk of myself. I believe I think less than I talk, but the subject is growing stale; as those who are long dying feel, I dare say—if they do not take it as the compensation for their departure.'

The Bull's Head, or British Jury of Twelve, with the wig on it, was faced during the latter half of a week of good news. First, Mr. Thomas Redworth was returned to Parliament by a stout majority for the Borough of Orrybridge: the Hon. Percy Dacier delivered a brilliant speech in the House of Commons, necessarily pleasing to his uncle: Lord Larrian obtained the command of the Rock: the house of The Crossways was let to a tenant approved by Mr. Braddock: Diana received the opening proof- sheets of her little volume, and an instalment of the modest honorarium: and finally, the Plaintiff in the suit involving her name was adjudged to have not proved his charge.

She heard of it without a change of countenance.

She could not have wished it the reverse; she was exonerated. But she was not free; far from that; and she revenged herself on the friends who made much of her triumph and overlooked her plight, by showing no sign of satisfaction. There was in her bosom a revolt at the legal consequences of the verdict—or blunt acquiescence of the Law in the conditions possibly to be imposed on her unless she went straight to the relieving phial; and the burden of keeping it under, set her wildest humour alight, somewhat as Redworth remembered of her on the journey from The Crossways to Copsley. This ironic fury, coming of the contrast of the outer and the inner, would have been indulged to the extent of permanent injury to her disposition had not her beloved Emma, immediately after the tension of the struggle ceased, required her tenderest aid. Lady Dunstane chanted victory, and at night collapsed. By the advice of her physician she was removed to Copsley, where Diana's labour of anxious nursing restored her through love to a saner spirit. The hopefulness of life must bloom again in the heart whose prayers are offered for a life dearer than its own to be preserved. A little return of confidence in Sir Lukin also refreshed her when she saw that the poor creature did honestly, in his shaggy rough male fashion, reverence and cling to the flower of souls he named as his wife. His piteous groans of self-accusation during the crisis haunted her, and made the conduct and nature of men a bewilderment to her still young understanding. Save for the knot of her sensations (hardly a mental memory, but a sullen knot) which she did not disentangle to charge him with his complicity in the blind rashness of her marriage, she might have felt sisterly, as warmly as she compassionated him.

It was midwinter when Dame Gossip, who keeps the exotic world alive with her fanning whispers, related that the lovely Mrs. Warwick had left England on board the schooner-yacht Clarissa, with Lord and Lady Esquart, for a voyage in the Mediterranean: and (behind her hand) that the reason was urgent, inasmuch as she fled to escape the meshes of the terrific net of the marital law brutally whirled to capture her by the man her husband.

CHAPTER XV.
INTRODUCES THE HON. PERCY DACIER

The Gods of this world's contests, against whom our poor stripped individual is commonly in revolt, are, as we know, not miners, they are reapers; and if we appear no longer on the surface, they cease to bruise us: they will allow an arena character to be cleansed and made presentable while enthusiastic friends preserve discretion. It is of course less than magnanimity; they are not proposed to you for your worship; they are little Gods, temporary as that great wave, their parent human mass of the hour. But they have one worshipful element in them, which is, the divine insistency upon there being two sides to a case —to every case. And the People so far directed by them may boast of healthfulness. Let the individual shriek, the innocent, triumphant, have in honesty to admit the fact. One side is vanquished, according to decree of Law, but the superior Council does not allow it to be extinguished.

Diana's battle was fought shadowily behind her for the space of a week or so, with some advocates on behalf of the beaten man; then it became a recollection of a beautiful woman, possibly erring, misvalued by a husband, who was neither a man of the world nor a gracious yokefellow, nor anything to match her. She, however, once out of the public flames, had to recall her scorchings to be gentle with herself. Under a defeat, she would have been angrily self-vindicated. The victory of the ashen laurels drove her mind inward to gird at the hateful yoke, in compassion for its pair of victims. Quite earnestly by such means, yet always bearing a comical eye on her subterfuges, she escaped the extremes of personal blame. Those advocates of her opponent in and out of court compelled her honest heart to search within and own to faults. But were they not natural faults? It was her marriage; it was marriage in the abstract: her own mistake and the world's clumsy machinery of civilization: these were the capital offenders: not the wife who would laugh ringingly, and would have friends of the other sex, and shot her epigrams at the helpless despot, and was at times—yes, vixenish; a nature driven to it, but that was the word. She was too generous to recount her charges against the vanquished. If his wretched jealousy had ruined her, the secret high tribunal within her bosom, which judged her guiltless for putting the sword between their marriage tie when they stood as one, because a quarrelling couple could not in honour play the embracing, pronounced him just pardonable. She distinguished that he could only suppose, manlikely, one bad cause for the division.

To this extent she used her unerring brains, more openly than on her night of debate at The Crossways. The next moment she was off in vapour, meditating grandly on her independence of her sex and the passions. Love! she did not know it, she was not acquainted with either the criminal or the domestic God, and persuaded herself that she never could be. She was a Diana of coldness, preferring friendship; she could be the friend of men. There was another who could be the friend of women. Her heart leapt to Redworth. Conjuring up his clear trusty face, at their grasp of hands when parting, she thought of her visions of her future about the period of the Dublin Ball, and acknowledged, despite the erratic step to wedlock, a gain in having met and proved so true a friend. His face, figure, character, lightest look, lightest word, all were loyal signs of a man of honour, cold as she; he was the man to whom she could have opened her heart for inspection. Rejoicing in her independence of an emotional sex, the impulsive woman burned with a regret that at their parting she had not broken down conventional barriers and given her cheek to his lips in the antiinsular fashion with a brotherly friend. And why not when both were cold? Spirit to spirit, she did, delightfully refreshed by her capacity to do so without a throb. He had held her hands and looked into her eyes half a minute, like a dear comrade; as little arousing her instincts of defensiveness as the clearing heavens; and sisterly love for it was his due, a sister's kiss. He needed a sister, and should have one in her. Emma's recollected talk of 'Tom Redworth' painted him from head to foot, brought the living man over the waters to the deck of the yacht. A stout champion in the person of Tom Redworth was left on British land; but for some reason past analysis, intermixed, that is, among a swarm of sensations, Diana named her champion to herself with the formal prefix: perhaps because she knew a man's Christian name to be dangerous handling. They differed besides frequently in opinion, when the habit of thinking of him as Mr. Redworth would be best. Women are bound to such small observances, and especially the beautiful of the sisterhood, whom the world soon warns that they carry explosives and must particularly guard against the ignition of petty sparks. She was less indiscreet in her thoughts than in her acts, as is the way with the reflective daughter of impulse; though she had fine mental distinctions: what she could offer to do 'spirit to spirit,' for instance, held nothing to her mind of the intimacy of calling the gentleman plain Tom in mere contemplation of him. Her friend and champion was a volunteer, far from a mercenary, and he deserved the reward, if she could bestow it unalarmed. They were to meet in Egypt. Meanwhile England loomed the home of hostile forces ready to shock, had she been a visible planet, and ready to secrete a virus of her past history, had she been making new.

She was happily away, borne by a whiter than swan's wing on the sapphire Mediterranean. Her letters to Emma were peeps of splendour for the invalid: her way of life on board the yacht, and sketches of her host and hostess as lovers in wedlock on the other side of our perilous forties; sketches of the bays, the towns, the people-priests, dames, cavaliers, urchins, infants, shifting groups of supple southerners-flashed across the page like a web of silk, and were dashed off, redolent of herself, as lightly as the silvery spray of the blue waves she furrowed; telling, without allusions to the land behind her, that she had dipped in the wells of blissful oblivion. Emma Dunstane, as is usual with those who receive exhilarating correspondence from makers of books, condemned the authoress in comparison, and now first saw that she had the gift of writing. Only one cry: 'Italy, Eden of exiles!' betrayed the seeming of a moan. She wrote of her poet and others immediately. Thither had they fled; with adieu to England!

How many have waved the adieu! And it is England nourishing, England protecting them, England clothing them in the honours they wear. Only the posturing lower natures, on the level of their buskins, can pluck out the pocket-knife of sentimental spite to cut themselves loose from her at heart in earnest. The higher, bleed as they may, too pressingly feel their debt. Diana had the Celtic vivid sense of country. In England she was Irish, by hereditary, and by wilful opposition. Abroad, gazing along the waters, observing, comparing, reflecting, above all, reading of the struggles at home, the things done and attempted, her soul of generosity made her, though not less Irish, a daughter of Britain. It is at a distance that striving countries should be seen if we would have them in the pure idea; and this young woman of fervid mind, a reader of public speeches and speculator on the tides of politics (desirous, further, to feel herself rather more in the pure idea), began to yearn for England long before her term of holiday exile had ended. She had been flattered by her friend, her 'wedded martyr at the stake,' as she named him, to believe that she could exercise a judgement in politics—could think, even speak acutely, on public affairs. The reports of speeches delivered by the men she knew or knew of, set her thrilling; and she fancied the sensibility to be as independent of her sympathy with the orators as her political notions were sovereignty above a sex devoted to trifles, and the feelings of a woman who had gone through fire. She fancied it confidently, notwithstanding a peculiar intuition that the plunge into the nobler business of the world would be a haven of safety for a woman with blood and imagination, when writing to Emma: 'Mr. Redworth's great success in Parliament is good in itself, whatever his views of present questions; and I do not heed them when I look to what may be done by a man of such power in striking at unjust laws, which keep the really numerically better-half of the population in a state of slavery. If he had been a lawyer! It must be a lawyer's initiative—a lawyer's Bill. Mr. Percy Dacier also spoke well, as might have been expected, and his uncle's compliment to him was merited. Should you meet him sound him. He has read for the Bar, and is younger than Mr. Redworth. The very young men and the old are our hope. The middleaged are hard and fast for existing facts. We pick our leaders on the slopes, the incline and decline of the mountain—not on the upper table-land midway, where all appears to men so solid, so tolerably smooth, save for a few excrescences, roughnesses, gradually to be levelled at their leisure; which induces one to protest that the middle-age of men is their time of delusion. It is no paradox. They may be publicly useful in a small way. I do not deny it at all. They must be near the gates of life—the opening or the closing—for their minds to be accessible to the urgency of the greater questions. Otherwise the world presents itself to them under too settled an aspect—unless, of course, Vesuvian Revolution shakes the land. And that touches only their nerves. I dream of some old Judge! There is one—if having caught we could keep him. But I dread so tricksy a pilot. You have guessed him—the ancient Puck! We have laughed all day over the paper telling us of his worrying the Lords. Lady Esquart congratulates her husband on being out of it. Puck 'biens ride' and bewigged might perhaps—except that at the critical moment he would be sure to plead allegiance to Oberon. However, the work will be performed by some one: I am prophetic:—when maidens are grandmothers!—when your Tony is wearing a perpetual laugh in the unhusbanded regions where there is no institution of the wedding-tie.'

For the reason that she was not to participate in the result of the old Judge's or young hero's happy championship of the cause of her sex, she conceived her separateness high aloof, and actually supposed she was a contemplative, simply speculative political spirit, impersonal albeit a woman. This, as Emma, smiling at the lines, had not to learn, was always her secret pride of fancy—the belief in her possession of a disengaged intellect.

The strange illusion, so clearly exposed to her correspondent, was maintained through a series of letters very slightly descriptive, dated from the Piraeus, the Bosphorus, the coasts of the Crimea, all more or less relating to the latest news of the journals received on board the yacht, and of English visitors fresh from the country she now seemed fond of calling 'home.' Politics, and gentle allusions to the curious exhibition of 'love in marriage' shown by her amiable host and hostess: 'these dear Esquarts, who are never tired of one another, but courtly courting, tempting me to think it possible that a fortunate selection and a mutual deference may subscribe to human happiness:—filled the paragraphs. Reviews of her first literary venture were mentioned once: 'I was well advised by Mr. Redworth in putting ANTONIA for authoress. She is a buff jerkin to the stripes, and I suspect that the signature of D. E. M., written in full, would have cawed woefully to hear that her style is affected, her characters nullities, her cleverness forced, etc., etc. As it is, I have much the same contempt for poor Antonia's performance. Cease penning, little fool! She writes, "with some comprehension of the passion of love." I know her to be a stranger to the earliest cry. So you see, dear, that utter ignorance is the mother of the Art. Dialogues "occasionally pointed." She has a sister who may do better.—But why was I not apprenticed to a serviceable profession or a trade? I perceive now that a hanger-on of the market had no right to expect a happier fate than mine has been.'

On the Nile, in the winter of the year, Diana met the Hon. Percy Dacier. He was introduced to her at Cairo by Redworth. The two gentlemen had struck up a House of Commons acquaintanceship, and finding themselves bound for the same destination, had grown friendly. Redworth's arrival had been pleasantly expected. She remarked on Dacier's presence to Emma, without sketch or note of him as other than much esteemed by Lord and Lady Esquart. These, with Diana, Redworth, Dacier, the German Eastern traveller Schweizerbarth, and the French Consul and Egyptologist Duriette, composed a voyaging party up the river, of which expedition Redworth was Lady Dunstane's chief writer of the records. His novel perceptiveness and shrewdness of touch made them amusing; and his tenderness to the Beauty's coquettry between the two foreign rivals, moved a deeper feeling. The German had a guitar, the Frenchman a voice; Diana joined them in harmony. They complained apart severally of the accompaniment and the singer. Our English criticized them apart; and that is at any rate to occupy a post, though it contributes nothing to entertainment. At home the Esquarts had sung duets; Diana had assisted Redworth's manly chest-notes at the piano. Each of them declined to be vocal. Diana sang alone for the credit of the country, Italian and French songs, Irish also. She was in her mood of Planxty Kelly and Garryowen all the way. 'Madame est Irlandaise?' Redworth heard the Frenchman say, and he owned to what was implied in the answering tone of the question. 'We should be dull dogs without the Irish leaven!' So Tony in exile still managed to do something for her darling Erin. The solitary woman on her heights at Copsley raised an exclamation of, 'Oh! that those two had been or could be united!' She was conscious of a mystic symbolism in the prayer.

She was not apprehensive of any ominous intervention of another. Writing from Venice, Diana mentioned Mr. Percy Dacier as being engaged to an heiress; 'A Miss Asper, niece of a mighty shipowner, Mr. Quintin Manx, Lady Esquart tells me: money fabulous, and necessary to a younger son devoured with ambition. The elder brother, Lord Creedmore, is a common Nimrod, always absent in Hungary, Russia, America, hunting somewhere. Mr. Dacier will be in the Cabinet with the next Ministry.' No more of him. A new work by ANTONIA was progressing.

The Summer in South Tyrol passed like a royal procession before young eyes for Diana, and at the close of it, descending the Stelvio, idling through the Valtelline, Como Lake was reached, Diana full of her work, living the double life of the author. At Bellagio one afternoon Mr. Percy Dacier appeared. She remembered subsequently a disappointment she felt in not beholding Mr. Redworth either with him or displacing him. If engaged to a lady, he was not an ardent suitor; nor was he a pointedly complimentary acquaintance. His enthusiasm was reserved for Italian scenery. She had already formed a sort of estimate of his character, as an indifferent observer may do, and any woman previous to the inflaming of her imagination, if that is in store for her; and she now fell to work resetting the puzzle it became as soon her positive conclusions had to be shaped again. 'But women never can know young men,' she wrote to Emma, after praising his good repute as one of the brotherhood. 'He drops pretty sentences now and then: no compliments; milky nuts. Of course he has a head, or he would not be where he is—and that seems always to me the most enviable place a young man can occupy.' She observed in him a singular conflicting of a buoyant animal nature with a curb of studiousness, as if the fardels of age were piling on his shoulders before youth had quitted its pastures.

His build of limbs and his features were those of the finely-bred English; he had the English taste for sports, games, manly diversions; and in the bloom of life, under thirty, his head was given to bend. The head bending on a tall upright figure, where there was breadth of chest, told of weights working. She recollected his open look, larger than inquiring, at the introduction to her; and it recurred when she uttered anything specially taking. What it meant was past a guess, though comparing it with the frank directness of Redworth's eyes, she saw the difference between a look that accepted her and one that dilated on two opinions.

Her thought of the gentleman was of a brilliant young charioteer in the ruck of the race, watchful for his chance to push to the front; and she could have said that a dubious consort might spoil a promising career. It flattered her to think that she sometimes prompted him, sometimes illumined. He repeated sentences she had spoken. 'I shall be better able to describe Mr. Dacier when you and I sit together, my Emmy, and a stroke here and there completes the painting. Set descriptions are good for puppets. Living men and women are too various in the mixture fashioning them—even the "external presentment"—to be livingly rendered in a formal sketch. I may tell you his eyes are pale blue, his features regular, his hair silky, brownish, his legs long, his head rather stooping (only the head), his mouth commonly closed; these are the facts, and you have seen much the same in a nursery doll. Such literary craft is of the nursery. So with landscapes. The art of the pen (we write on darkness) is to rouse the inward vision, instead of labouring with a Drop-scene brush, as if it were to the eye; because our flying minds cannot contain a protracted description. That is why the poets, who spring imagination with a word or a phrase, paint lasting pictures. The Shakespearian, the Dantesque, are in a line, two at most. He lends an attentive ear when I speak, agrees or has a quaint pucker of the eyebrows dissenting inwardly. He lacks mental liveliness—cheerfulness, I should say, and is thankful to have it imparted. One suspects he would be a dull domestic companion. He has a veritable thirst for hopeful views of the world, and no spiritual distillery of his own. He leans to depression. Why! The broken reed you call your Tony carries a cargo, all of her manufacture—she reeks of secret stills; and here is a young man—a sapling oak—inclined to droop. His nature has an air of imploring me que je d'arrose! I begin to perform Mrs. Dr. Pangloss on purpose to brighten him—the mind, the views. He is not altogether deficient in conversational gaiety, and he shines in exercise. But the world is a poor old ball bounding down a hill—to an Irish melody in the evening generally, by request. So far of Mr. Percy Dacier, of whom I have some hopes—distant, perhaps delusive—that he may be of use to our cause. He listens. It is an auspicious commencement.'

Lugano is the Italian lake most lovingly encircled by mountain arms, and every height about it may be scaled with esce. The heights have their nest of waters below for a home scene, the southern Swiss peaks, with celestial Monta Rosa, in prospect. It was there that Diana reawakened, after the trance of a deadly draught, to the glory of the earth and her share in it. She wakened like the Princess of the Kiss; happily not to kisses; to no sign, touch or call that she could trace backward. The change befell her without a warning. After writing deliberately to her friend Emma, she laid down her pen and thought of nothing; and into this dreamfulness a wine passed, filling her veins, suffusing her mind, quickening her soul: and coming whence? out of air, out of the yonder of air. She could have imagined a seraphic presence in the room, that bade her arise and live; take the cup of the wells of youth arrested at her lips by her marriage; quit her wintry bondage for warmth, light, space, the quick of simple being. And the strange pure ecstasy was not a transient electrification; it came in waves on a continuous tide; looking was living; walking flying. She hardly knew that she slept. The heights she had seen rosy at eve were marked for her ascent in the dawn. Sleep was one wink, and fresh as the dewy field and rockflowers on her way upward, she sprang to more and more of heaven, insatiable, happily chirruping over her possessions. The threading of the town among the dear common people before others were abroad, was a pleasure and pleasant her solitariness threading the gardens at the base of the rock, only she astir; and the first rough steps of the winding footpath, the first closed buds, the sharper air, the uprising of the mountain with her ascent; and pleasant too was her hunger and the nibble at a little loaf of bread. A linnet sang in her breast, an eagle lifted her feet. The feet were verily winged, as they are in a season of youth when the blood leaps to light from the pressure of the under forces, like a source at the wellheads, and the whole creature blooms, vital in every energy as a spirit. To be a girl again was magical. She could fancy her having risen from the dead. And to be a girl, with a woman's broader vision and receptiveness of soul, with knowledge of evil, and winging to ethereal happiness, this was a revelation of our human powers.

She attributed the change to the influences of nature's beauty and grandeur. Nor had her woman's consciousness to play the chrysalis in any shy recesses of her heart; she was nowhere veiled or torpid; she was illumined, like the Salvatore she saw in the evening beams and mounted in the morning's; and she had not a spot of seeresy; all her nature flew and bloomed; she was bird, flower, flowing river, a quivering sensibility unweighted, enshrouded. Desires and hopes would surely have weighted and shrouded her. She had none, save for the upper air, the eyes of the mountain.

Which was the dream—her past life or this ethereal existence? But this ran spontaneously, and the other had often been stimulated—

her vivaciousness on the Nile-boat, for a recent example. She had not a doubt that her past life was the dream, or deception: and for the reason that now she was compassionate, large of heart toward all beneath her. Let them but leave her free, they were forgiven, even to prayers for their well-being! The plural number in the case was an involuntary multiplying of the single, coming of her incapacity during this elevation and rapture of the senses to think distinctly of that One who had discoloured her opening life. Freedom to breathe, gaze, climb, grow with the grasses, fly with the clouds, to muse, to sing, to be an unclaimed self, dispersed upon earth, air, sky, to find a keener transfigured self in that radiation—she craved no more.

Bear in mind her beauty, her charm of tongue, her present state of white simplicity in fervour: was there ever so perilous a woman for the most guarded and clearest-eyed of young men to meet at early morn upon a mountain side?

CHAPTER XVI.
TREATS OF A MIDNIGHT BELL, AND OF A SCENE OF EARLY MORNING

On a round of the mountains rising from Osteno, South eastward of Lugano, the Esquart party rose from the natural grotto and headed their carriages up and down the defiles, halting for a night at Rovio, a little village below the Generoso, lively with waterfalls and watercourses; and they fell so in love with the place, that after roaming along the flowery borderways by moonlight, they resolved to rest there two or three days and try some easy ascents. In the diurnal course of nature, being pleasantly tired, they had the avowed intention of sleeping there; so they went early to their beds, and carelessly wished one another good- night, none of them supposing slumber to be anywhere one of the warlike arts, a paradoxical thing you must battle for and can only win at last when utterly beaten. Hard by their inn, close enough for a priestly homily to have been audible, stood a church campanile, wherein hung a Bell, not ostensibly communicating with the demons of the pit; in daylight rather a merry comrade. But at night, when the children of nerves lay stretched, he threw off the mask. As soon as they had fairly nestled, he smote their pillows a shattering blow, loud for the retold preluding quarters, incredibly clanging the number ten. Then he waited for neighbouring campanili to box the ears of slumber's votaries in turn; whereupon, under pretence of excessive conscientiousness, or else oblivious of his antecedent, damnable misconduct, or perhaps in actual league and trapdoor conspiracy with the surging goblin hosts beneath us, he resumed his blaring strokes, a sonorous recapitulation of the number; all the others likewise. It was an alarum fit to warn of Attila or Alaric; and not, simply the maniacal noise invaded the fruitful provinces of sleep like Hun and Vandal, the irrational repetition ploughed the minds of those unhappy somnivolents, leaving them worse than sheared by barbarians, disrupt, as by earthquake, with the unanswerable question to Providence, Why!—Why twice?

Designing slumberers are such infants. When they have undressed and stretched themselves, flat, it seems that they have really gone back to their mothers' breasts, and they fret at whatsoever does not smack of nature, or custom. The cause of a repetition so senseless in its violence, and so unnecessary, set them querying and kicking until the inevitable quarters recommenced. Then arose an insurgent rabble in their bosoms, it might be the loosened imps of darkness, urging them to speculate whether the proximate monster about to dole out the eleventh hour in uproar would again forget himself and repeat his dreary arithmetic a second time; for they were unaware of his religious obligation, following the hour of the district, to inform them of the tardy hour of Rome. They waited in suspense, curiosity enabling them to bear the first crash callously. His performance was the same. And now they took him for a crazy engine whose madness had infected the whole neighbourhood. Now was the moment to fight for sleep in contempt of him, and they began by simulating an entry into the fortress they were to defend, plunging on their pillows, battening down their eyelids, breathing with a dreadful regularity. Alas! it came to their knowledge that the Bell was in possession and they the besiegers. Every resonant quarter was anticipated up to the blow, without averting its murderous abruptness; and an executioner Midnight that sounded, in addition to the reiterated quarters, four and twenty ringing hammerstrokes, with the aching pause between the twelves, left them the prey of the legions of torturers which are summed, though not described, in the title of a sleepless night.

From that period the curse was milder, but the victims raged. They swam on vasty deeps, they knocked at rusty gates, they shouldered all the weapons of black Insomnia's armoury and became her soldiery, doing her will upon themselves. Of her originally sprang the inspired teaching of the doom of men to excruciation in endlessness. She is the fountain of the infinite ocean whereon the exceedingly sensitive soul is tumbled everlastingly, with the diversion of hot pincers to appease its appetite for change.

Dacier was never the best of sleepers. He had taken to exercise his brains prematurely, not only in learning, but also in reflection; and a reflectiveness that is indulged before we have a rigid mastery of the emotions, or have slain them, is apt to make a young man more than commonly a child of nerves: nearly as much so as the dissipated, with the difference that they are hilarious while wasting their treasury, which he is not; and he may recover under favouring conditions, which is a point of vantage denied to them. Physically he had stout reserves, for he had not disgraced the temple. His intemperateness lay in the craving to rise and lead: a precocious ambition. This apparently modest young man started with an aim—and if in the distance and with but a slingstone, like the slender shepherd fronting the Philistine, all his energies were in his aim—at Government. He had hung on the fringe of an Administration. His party was out, and he hoped for higher station on its return to power. Many perplexities were therefore buzzing about his head; among them at present one sufficiently magnified and voracious to swallow the remainder. He added force to the interrogation as to why that Bell should sound its inhuman strokes twice, by asking himself why he was there to hear it! A strange suspicion of a bewitchment might have enlightened him if he had been a man accustomed to yield to the peculiar kind of sorcery issuing from that sex. He rather despised the power of women over men: and nevertheless he was there, listening to that Bell, instead of having obeyed the call of his family duties, when the latter were urgent. He had received letters at Lugano, summoning him home, before he set forth on his present expedition. The noisy alarum told him he floundered in quags, like a silly creature chasing a marsh-lamp. But was it so? Was it not, on the contrary, a serious pursuit of the secret of a woman's character?—Oh, a woman and her character! Ordinary women and their characters might set to work to get what relationship and likeness they could. They had no secret to allure. This one had: she had the secret of lake waters under rock, unfathomable in limpidness. He could not think of her without shooting at nature, and nature's very sweetest and subtlest, for comparison. As to her sex, his active man's contempt of the petticoated secret attractive to boys and graylings, made him believe that in her he hunted the mind and the spirit: perchance a double mind, a twilighted spirit; but not a mere woman. She bore no resemblance to the bundle of women. Well, she was worth studying; she had ideas, and could give ear to ideas. Furthermore, a couple of the members of his family inclined to do her injustice. At least, they judged her harshly, owing, he thought, to an inveterate opinion they held regarding Lord Dannisburgh's obliquity in relation to women. He shared it, and did not concur in, their verdict upon the woman implicated. That is to say, knowing something of her now, he could see the possibility of her innocence in the special charm that her mere sparkle of features and speech, and her freshness would have for a man like his uncle. The possibility pleaded strongly on her behalf, while the darker possibility weighted by his uncle's reputation plucked at him from below.

She was delightful to hear, delightful to see; and her friends loved her and had faith in her. So clever a woman might be too clever for her friends! . . .

The circle he moved in hummed of women, prompting novices as well as veterans to suspect that the multitude of them, and notably the fairest, yet more the cleverest, concealed the serpent somewhere.

She certainly had not directed any of her arts upon him. Besides he was half engaged. And that was a burning perplexity; not because of abstract scruples touching the necessity for love in marriage. The young lady, great heiress though she was, and willing, as she allowed him to assume; graceful too, reputed a beauty; struck him cold. He fancied her transparent, only Arctic. Her transparency displayed to him all the common virtues, and a serene possession of the inestimable and eminent one outweighing all; but charm, wit, ardour, intercommunicative quickness, and kindling beauty, airy grace, were qualities that a man, it seemed, had to look for in women spotted by a doubt of their having the chief and priceless.

However, he was not absolutely plighted. Nor did it matter to him whether this or that woman concealed the tail of the serpent and trail, excepting the singular interest this woman managed to excite, and so deeply as set him wondering how that Resurrection Bell might be affecting her ability to sleep. Was she sleeping?—or waking? His nervous imagination was a torch that alternately lighted her lying asleep with the innocent, like a babe, and tossing beneath the overflow of her dark hair, hounded by haggard memories. She fluttered before him in either aspect; and another perplexity now was to distinguish within himself which was the aspect he preferred. Great Nature brought him thus to drink of her beauty, under the delusion that the act was a speculation on her character.

The Bell, with its clash, throb and long swoon of sound, reminded him of her name: Diana!—An attribute? or a derision?

It really mattered nothing to him, save for her being maligned; and if most unfairly, then that face of the varying expressions, and the rich voice, and the remembered gentle and taking words coming from her, appealed to him with a supplicating vividness that pricked his heart to leap.

He was dozing when the Bell burst through the thin division between slumber and wakefulness, recounting what seemed innumerable peals, hard on his cranium. Gray daylight blanched the window and the bed: his watch said five of the morning. He thought of the pleasure of a bath beneath some dashing spray-showers; and jumped up to dress, feeling a queer sensation of skin in his clothes, the sign of a feverish night; and yawning he went into the air. Leftward the narrow village street led to the footway along which he could make for the mountain-wall. He cast one look at the head of the campanile, silly as an owlish roysterer's glazed stare at the young Aurora, and hurried his feet to check the yawns coming alarmingly fast, in the place of ideas.

His elevation above the valley was about the kneecap of the Generoso. Waters of past rain-clouds poured down the mountain-sides like veins of metal, here and there flinging off a shower on the busy descent; only dubiously animate in the lack lustre of the huge bulk piled against a yellow East that wafted fleets of pinky cloudlets overhead. He mounted his path to a level with inviting grassmounds where water circled, running from scoops and cups to curves and brook-streams, and in his fancy calling to him to hear them. To dip in them was his desire. To roll and shiver braced by the icy flow was the spell to break that baleful incantation of the intolerable night; so he struck across a ridge of boulders, wreck of a landslip from the height he had hugged, to the open space of shadowed undulations, and soon had his feet on turf. Heights to right and to left, and between them, aloft, a sky the rosy wheelcourse of the chariot of morn, and below, among the knolls, choice of sheltered nooks where waters whispered of secresy to satisfy Diana herself. They have that whisper and waving of secresy in secret scenery; they beckon to the bath; and they conjure classic visions of the pudency of the Goddess irate or unsighted. The semi-mythological state of mind, built of old images and favouring haunts, was known to Dacier. The name of Diana, playing vaguely on his consciousness, helped to it. He had no definite thought of the mortal woman when the highest grass-roll near the rock gave him view of a bowered source and of a pool under a chain of cascades, bounded by polished shelves and slabs. The very spot for him, he decided at the first peep; and at the second, with fingers instinctively loosening his waist-coat buttons for a commencement, he shouldered round and strolled away, though not at a rapid pace, nor far before he halted.

That it could be no other than she, the figure he had seen standing beside the pool, he was sure. Why had he turned? Thoughts thick and swift as a blush in the cheeks of seventeen overcame him; and queen of all, the thought bringing the picture of this mountain-solitude to vindicate a woman shamefully assailed. —She who found her pleasure in these haunts of nymph and Goddess, at the fresh cold bosom of nature, must be clear as day. She trusted herself to the loneliness here, and to the honour of men, from a like irreflective sincereness. She was unable to imagine danger where her own impelling thirst was pure. . .

The thoughts, it will be discerned, were but flashes of a momentary vivid sensibility. Where a woman's charm has won half the battle, her character is an advancing standard and sings victory, let her do no more than take a quiet morning walk before breakfast.

But why had he turned his back on her? There was nothing in his presence to alarm, nothing in her appearance to forbid. The motive and the movement were equally quaint; incomprehensible to him; for after putting himself out of sight, he understood the absurdity of the supposition that she would seek the secluded sylvan bath for the same purpose as he. Yet now he was, debarred from going to meet her. She might have an impulse to bathe her feet. Her name was Diana . . . .

Yes, and a married woman; and a proclaimed one!

And notwithstanding those brassy facts, he was ready to side with the evidence declaring her free from stain; and further, to swear that her blood was Diana's!

Nor had Dacier ever been particularly poetical about women. The present Diana had wakened his curiosity, had stirred his interest in her, pricked his admiration, but gradually, until a sleepless night with its flock of raven-fancies under that dominant Bell, ended by colouring her, the moment she stood in his eyes, as freshly as the morning heavens. We are much influenced in youth by sleepless nights: they disarm, they predispose us to submit to soft occasion; and in our youth occasion is always coming.

He heard her voice. She had risen up the grass-mound, and he hung brooding half-way down. She was dressed in some texture of the hue of lavender. A violet scarf loosely knotted over the bosom opened on her throat. The loop of her black hair curved under a hat of gray beaver. Memorably radiant was her face.

They met, exchanged greetings, praised the beauty of the morning, and struck together on the Bell. She laughed: 'I heard it at ten; I slept till four. I never wake later. I was out in the air by half-past. Were you disturbed?'

He alluded to his troubles with the Bell.

'It sounded like a felon's heart in skeleton ribs,' he said.

'Or a proser's tongue in a hollow skull,' said she.

He bowed to her conversible readiness, and at once fell into the background, as he did only with her, to perform accordant bass in their dialogue; for when a woman lightly caps our strained remarks, we gallantly surrender the leadership, lest she should too cuttingly assert her claim.

Some sweet wild cyclamen flowers were at her breast. She held in her left hand a bunch of buds and blown cups of the pale purple meadow- crocus. He admired them. She told him to look round. He confessed to not having noticed them in the grass: what was the name? Colchicum, in Botany, she said.

'These are plucked to be sent to a friend; otherwise I'm reluctant to take the life of flowers for a whim. Wild flowers, I mean. I am not sentimental about garden flowers: they are cultivated for decoration, grown for clipping.'

'I suppose they don't carry the same signification,' said Dacier, in the tone of a pupil to such themes.

'They carry no feeling,' said she. 'And that is my excuse for plucking these, where they seem to spring like our town-dream of happiness. I believe they are sensible of it too; but these must do service to my invalid friend, who cannot travel. Are you ever as much interested in the woes of great ladies as of country damsels? I am not—not unless they have natural distinction. You have met Lady Dunstane?'

The question sounded artless. Dacier answered that he thought he had seen her somewhere once, and Diana shut her lips on a rising under-smile.

'She is the coeur d'or of our time; the one soul I would sacrifice these flowers to.'

'A bit of a blue-stocking, I think I have heard said.'

'She might have been admitted to the Hotel Rambouillet, without being anything of a Precieuse. She is the woman of the largest heart now beating.'

'Mr. Redworth talked of her.'

'As she deserved, I am sure.'

'Very warmly.'

'He would!'

'He told me you were the Damon and Pythias of women.'

'Her one fault is an extreme humility that makes her always play second to me; and as I am apt to gabble, I take the lead; and I am froth in comparison. I can reverence my superiors even when tried by intimacy with them. She is the next heavenly thing to heaven that I know. Court her, if ever you come across her. Or have you a man's horror of women with brains?'

'Am I expressing it?' said he.

'Do not breathe London or Paris here on me.' She fanned the crocuses under her chin. 'The early morning always has this—I wish I had a word!—touch . . . whisper . . . gleam . . . beat of wings—I envy poets now more than ever!—of Eden, I was going to say. Prose can paint evening and moonlight, but poets are needed to sing the dawn. That is because prose is equal to melancholy stuff. Gladness requires the finer language. Otherwise we have it coarse—anything but a reproduction. You politicians despise the little distinctions "twixt tweedledum and tweedledee," I fancy.'

Of the poetic sort, Dacier's uncle certainly did. For himself he confessed to not having thought much on them.

'But how divine is utterance!' she said. 'As we to the brutes, poets are to us.'

He listened somewhat with the head of the hanged. A beautiful woman choosing to rhapsodize has her way, and is not subjected to the critical commentary within us. He wondered whether she had discoursed in such a fashion to his uncle.

'I can read good poetry,' said he.

'If you would have this valley—or mountain-cleft, one should call it— described, only verse could do it for you,' Diana pursued, and stopped, glanced at his face, and smiled. She had spied the end of a towel peeping out of one of his pockets. 'You came out for a bath! Go back, by all means, and mount that rise of grass where you first saw me; and down on the other side, a little to the right, you will find the very place for a bath, at a corner of the rock—a natural fountain; a bubbling pool in a ring of brushwood, with falling water, so tempting that I could have pardoned a push: about five feet deep. Lose no time.'

He begged to assure her that he would rather stroll with her: it had been only a notion of bathing by chance when he pocketed the towel.

'Dear me,' she cried, 'if I had been a man I should have scurried off at a signal of release, quick as a hare I once woke up in a field with my foot on its back.'

Dacier's eyebrows knotted a trifle over her eagerness to dismiss him: he was not used to it, but rather to be courted by women, and to condescend.

'I shall not long, I'm afraid, have the pleasure of walking beside you and hearing you. I had letters at Lugano. My uncle is unwell, I hear.'

'Lord Dannisburgh?'

The name sprang from her lips unhesitatingly.

His nodded affirmative altered her face and her voice.

'It is not a grave illness?'

'They rather fear it.'

'You had the news at Lugano?'

He answered the implied reproach: 'I can be of no, service.'

'But surely!'

'It's even doubtful that he would be bothered to receive me. We hold no views in common—excepting one.'

'Could I?' she exclaimed. 'O that I might! If he is really ill ! But if it is actually serious he would perhaps have a wish . . . I can nurse.

I know I have the power to cheer him. You ought indeed to be in England.'

Dacier said he had thought it better to wait for later reports. 'I shall drive to Lugano this afternoon, and act on the information I get there. Probably it ends my holiday.'

'Will you do me the favour to write me word?—and especially tell me if you think he would like to have me near him,' said Diana. 'And let him know that if he wants nursing or cheerful companionship, I am at any moment ready to come.'

The flattery of a beautiful young woman to wait on him would be very agreeable to Lord Dannisburgh, Dacier conceived. Her offer to go was possibly purely charitable. But the prudence of her occupation of the post obscured whatever appeared admirable in her devotedness. Her choice of a man like Lord Dannisburgh for the friend to whom she could sacrifice her good name less falteringly than she gathered those field-flowers was inexplicable; and she herself a darker riddle at each step of his reading.

He promised curtly to write. 'I will do my best to hit a flying address.'

'Your Club enables me to hit a permanent one that will establish the communication,' said Diana. 'We shall not sleep another night at Rovio. Lady Esquart is the lightest of sleepers, and if you had a restless time, she and her husband must have been in purgatory. Besides, permit me to say, you should be with your party. The times are troublous—not for holidays! Your holiday has had a haunted look, creditably to your conscience as a politician. These Corn Law agitations!'

'Ah, but no politics here!' said Dacier.

'Politics everywhere!—in the Courts of Faery! They are not discord to me.'

'But not the last day—the last hour!' he pleaded.

'Well! only do not forget your assurance to me that you would give some thoughts to Ireland—and the cause of women. Has it slipped from your memory?'

'If I see the chance of serving you, you may trust to me.'

She sent up an interjection on the misfortune of her not having been born a man.

It was to him the one smart of sourness in her charm as a woman.

Among the boulder-stones of the ascent to the path, he ventured to propose a little masculine assistance in a hand stretched mutely. Although there was no great need for help, her natural kindliness checked the inclination to refuse it. When their hands disjoined she found herself reddening. She cast it on the exertion. Her heart was throbbing. It might be the exertion likewise.

He walked and talked much more airily along the descending pathway, as if he had suddenly become more intimately acquainted with her.

She listened, trying to think of the manner in which he might be taught to serve that cause she had at heart; and the colour deepened on her cheeks till it set fire to her underlying consciousness: blood to spirit. A tremour of alarm ran through her.

His request for one of the crocuses to keep as a souvenir of the morning was refused. 'They are sacred; they were all devoted to my friend when I plucked them.'

He pointed to a half-open one, with the petals in disparting pointing to junction, and compared it to the famous tiptoe ballet-posture, arms above head and fingers like swallows meeting in air, of an operatic danseuse of the time.

'I do not see it, because I will not see it,' she said, and she found a personal cooling and consolement in the phrase. — We have this power of resisting invasion of the poetic by the commonplace, the spirit by the blood, if we please, though you men may not think that we have! Her alarmed sensibilities bristled and made head against him as an enemy. She fancied (for the aforesaid reason—because she chose) that it was on account of the offence to her shy morning pleasure by his Londonizing. At any other moment her natural liveliness and trained social ease would have taken any remark on the eddies of the tide of converse; and so she told herself, and did not the less feel wounded, adverse, armed. He seemed somehow—to have dealt a mortal blow to the happy girl she had become again. The woman she was protested on behalf of the girl, while the girl in her heart bent lowered sad eyelids to the woman; and which of them was wiser of the truth she could not have said, for she was honestly not aware of the truth, but she knew she was divided in halves, with one half pitying the other, one rebuking: and all because of the incongruous comparison of a wild flower to an opera dancer! Absurd indeed. We human creatures are the silliest on earth, most certainly.

Dacier had observed the blush, and the check to her flowing tongue did not escape him as they walked back to the inn down the narrow street of black rooms, where the women gossiped at the fountain and the cobbler threaded on his doorstep. His novel excitement supplied the deficiency, sweeping him past minor reflections. He was, however, surprised to hear her tell Lady Esquart, as soon as they were together at the breakfast- table, that he had the intention of starting for England; and further surprised, and slightly stung too, when on the poor lady's, moaning over her recollection of the midnight Bell, and vowing she could not attempt to sleep another night in the place, Diana declared her resolve to stay there one day longer with her maid, and explore the neighbourhood for the wild flowers in which it abounded. Lord and Lady Esquart agreed to anything agreeable to her, after excusing themselves for the necessitated flight, piteously relating the story of their sufferings. My lord could have slept, but he had remained awake to comfort my lady.

'True knightliness!' Diana said, in praise of these long married lovers; and she asked them what they had talked of during the night.

'You, my dear, partly,' said Lady Esquart.

'For an opiate?'

'An invocation of the morning,' said Dacier.

Lady Esquart looked at Diana and, at him. She thought it was well that her fair friend should stay. It was then settled for Diana to rejoin them the next evening at Lugano, thence to proceed to Luino on the Maggiore.

'I fear it is good-bye for me,' Dacier said to her, as he was about to step into the carriage with the Esquarts.

'If you have not better news of your uncle, it must be,' she replied, and gave him her hand promptly and formally, hardly diverting her eyes from Lady Esquart to grace the temporary gift with a look. The last of her he saw was a waving of her arm and finger pointing triumphantly at the Bell in the tower. It said, to an understanding unpractised in the feminine mysteries: 'I can sleep through anything.' What that revealed of her state of conscience and her nature, his efforts to preserve the lovely optical figure blocked his guessing. He was with her friends, who liked her the more they knew her, and he was compelled to lean to their view of the perplexing woman.

'She is a riddle to the world,' Lady Esquart said, 'but I know that she is good. It is the best of signs when women take to her and are proud to be her friend.'

My lord echoed his wife. She talked in this homely manner to stop any notion of philandering that the young gentleman might be disposed to entertain in regard to a lady so attractive to the pursuit as Diana's beauty and delicate situation might make her seem.

'She is an exceedingly clever person, and handsomer than report, which is uncommon,' said Dacier, becoming voluble on town-topics, Miss Asper incidentally among them. He denied Lady Esquart's charge of an engagement; the matter hung.

His letters at Lugano summoned him to England instantly.

'I have taken leave of Mrs. Warwick, but tell her I regret, et caetera,' he said; 'and by the way, as my uncle's illness appears to be serious, the longer she is absent the better, perhaps.'

'It would never do,' said Lady Esquart, understanding his drift immediately. 'We winter in Rome. She will not abandon us—I have her word for it. Next Easter we are in Paris; and so home, I suppose. There will be no hurry before we are due at Cowes. We seem to have become confirmed wanderers; for two of us at least it is likely to be our last great tour.'

Dacier informed her that he had pledged his word to write to Mrs. Warwick of his uncle's condition, and the several appointed halting-places of the Esquarts between the lakes and Florence were named to him. Thus all things were openly treated; all had an air of being on the surface; the communications passing between Mrs. Warwick and the Hon. Percy Dacier might have been perused by all the world. None but that portion of it, sage in suspiciousness, which objects to such communications under any circumstances, could have detected in their correspondence a spark of coming fire or that there was common warmth. She did not feel it, nor did he. The position of the two interdicted it to a couple honourably sensible of social decencies; and who were, be it added, kept apart. The blood is the treacherous element in the story of the nobly civilized, of which secret

Diana, a wife and no wife, a prisoner in liberty, a blooming woman imagining herself restored to transcendent maiden ecstacies—the highest youthful poetic—had received some faint intimation when the blush flamed suddenly in her cheeks and her heart knelled like the towers of a city given over to the devourer. She had no wish to meet him again. Without telling herself why, she would have shunned the meeting. Disturbers that thwarted her simple happiness in sublime scenery were best avoided. She thought so the more for a fitful blur to the simplicity of her sensations, and a task she sometimes had in restoring and toning them, after that sweet morning time in Rovio.

CHAPTER XVII.
'THE PRINCESS EGERIA'

London, say what we will of it, is after all the head of the British giant, and if not the liveliest in bubbles, it is past competition the largest broth-pot of brains anywhere simmering on the hob: over the steadiest of furnaces too. And the oceans and the continents, as you know, are perpetual and copious contributors, either to the heating apparatus or to the contents of the pot. Let grander similes besought. This one fits for the smoky receptacle cherishing millions, magnetic to tens of millions more, with its caked outside of grime, and the inward substance incessantly kicking the lid, prankish, but never casting it off. A good stew, you perceive; not a parlous boiling. Weak as we may be in our domestic cookery, our political has been sagaciously adjusted as yet to catch the ardours of the furnace without being subject to their volcanic activities.

That the social is also somewhat at fault, we have proof in occasional outcries over the absence of these or those particular persons famous for inspiriting. It sticks and clogs. The improvising songster is missed, the convivial essayist, the humorous Dean, the travelled cynic, and he, the one of his day, the iridescent Irishman, whose remembered repartees are a feast, sharp and ringing, at divers tables descending from the upper to the fat citizen's, where, instead of coming in the sequence of talk, they are exposed by blasting, like fossil teeth of old Deluge sharks in monotonous walls of our chalk-quarries. Nor are these the less welcome for the violence of their introduction among a people glad to be set burning rather briskly awhile by the most unexpected of digs in the ribs. Dan Merion, to give an example. That was Dan Merion's joke with the watchman: and he said that other thing to the Marquis of Kingsbury, when the latter asked him if he had ever won a donkey-race. And old Dan is dead, and we are the duller for it! which leads to the question: Is genius hereditary? And the affirmative and negative are respectively maintained, rather against the Yes is the dispute, until a member of the audience speaks of Dan Merion's having left a daughter reputed for a sparkling wit not much below the level of his own. Why, are you unaware that the Mrs. Warwick of that scandal case of Warwick versus Dannisburgh was old Dan Merion's girl—and his only child? It is true; for a friend had it from a man who had it straight from Mr. Braddock, of the firm of Braddock, Thorpe and Simnel, her solicitors in the action, who told him he could sit listening to her for hours, and that she was as innocent as day; a wonderful combination of a good woman and a clever woman and a real beauty. Only her misfortune was to have a furiously jealous husband, and they say he went mad after hearing the verdict.

Diana was talked of in the London circles. A witty woman is such salt that where she has once been tasted she must perforce be missed more than any of the absent, the dowering heavens not having yet showered her like very plentifully upon us. Then it was first heard that Percy Dacier had been travelling with her. Miss Asper heard of it. Her uncle, Mr. Quintin Manx, the millionnaire, was an acquaintance of the new Judge and titled dignitary, Sir Cramborne Wathin, and she visited Lady Wathin, at whose table the report in the journals of the Nile-boat party was mentioned. Lady Wathin's table could dispense with witty women, and, for that matter, witty men. The intrusion of the spontaneous on the stereotyped would have clashed. She preferred, as hostess, the old legal anecdotes sure of their laugh, and the citations from the manufactories of fun in the Press, which were current and instantly intelligible to all her guests. She smiled suavely on an impromptu pun, because her experience of the humorous appreciation of it by her guests bade her welcome the upstart. Nothing else impromptu was acceptable. Mrs. Warwick therefore was not missed by Lady Wathin. 'I have met her,' she said. 'I confess I am not one of the fanatics about Mrs. Warwick. She has a sort of skill in getting men to clamour. If you stoop to tickle them, they will applaud. It is a way of winning a reputation.' When the ladies were separated from the gentlemen by the stream of Claret, Miss Asper heard Lady Wathin speak of Mrs. Warwick again. An allusion to Lord Dannisburgh's fit of illness in the House of Lords led to her saying that there was no doubt he had been fascinated, and that, in her opinion, Mrs. Warwick was a dangerous woman. Sir Cramborne knew something of Mr. Warwick; 'Poor man!' she added. A lady present put a question concerning Mrs. Warwick's beauty. 'Yes,' Lady Wathin said, 'she has good looks to aid her. Judging from what I hear and have seen, her thirst is for notoriety. Sooner or later we shall have her making a noise, you may be certain. Yes, she has the secret of dressing well—in the French style.'

A simple newspaper report of the expedition of a Nileboat party could stir the Powers to take her up and turn her on their wheel in this manner.

But others of the sons and daughters of London were regretting her prolonged absence. The great and exclusive Whitmonby, who had dined once at Lady Wathin's table, and vowed never more to repeat that offence to his patience, lamented bitterly to Henry Wilmers that the sole woman worthy of sitting at a little Sunday evening dinner with the cream of the choicest men of the time was away wasting herself in that insane modern chase of the picturesque! He called her a perverted Celimene.

Redworth had less to regret than the rest of her male friends, as he was receiving at intervals pleasant descriptive letters, besides manuscript sheets of ANTONIA'S new piece of composition, to correct the proofs for the press, and he read them critically, he thought. He read them with a watchful eye to guard them from the critics. ANTONIA, whatever her faults as a writer, was not one of the order whose Muse is the Public Taste. She did at least draw her inspiration from herself, and there was much to be feared in her work, if a sale was the object. Otherwise Redworth's highly critical perusal led him flatly to admire. This was like her, and that was like her, and here and there a phrase gave him the very play of her mouth, the flash of her eyes. Could he possibly wish, or bear, to, have anything altered? But she had reason to desire an extended sale of the work. Her aim, in the teeth of her independent style, was at the means of independence—a feminine method of attempting to conciliate contraries; and after despatching the last sheets to the printer, he meditated upon the several ways which might serve to, assist her; the main way running thus in his mind:—We have a work of genius. Genius is good for the public. What is good for the public should be recommended by the critics. It should be. How then to come at them to, get it done? As he was not a member of the honourable literary craft, and regarded its arcana altogether externally, it may be confessed of him that he deemed the Incorruptible corruptible;—not, of course, with filthy coin slid into sticky palms. Critics are human, and exceedingly, beyond the common lot, when touched; and they are excited by mysterious hints of loftiness in authorship; by rumours of veiled loveliness; whispers, of a general anticipation; and also Editors can jog them. Redworth was rising to be a Railway King of a period soon to glitter with rails, iron in the concrete, golden in the visionary. He had already his Court, much against his will. The powerful magnetic attractions of those who can help the world to fortune, was exercised by him in spite of his disgust of sycophants. He dropped words to right and left of a coming work by ANTONIA. And who was ANTONIA?— Ah! there hung the riddle.—An exalted personage?—So much so that he dared not name her even in confidence to ladies; he named the publishers. To men he said he was at liberty to speak of her only as the most beautiful woman of her time. His courtiers of both sexes were recommended to read the new story, THE PRINCESS EGERIA.

Oddly, one great lady of his Court had heard a forthcoming work of this title spoken of by Percy Dacier, not a man to read silly fiction, unless there was meaning behind the lines: that is, rich scandal of the aristocracy, diversified by stinging epigrams to the address of discernible personages. She talked of THE PRINCESS EGERIA: nay, laid her finger on the identical Princess. Others followed her. Dozens were soon flying with the torch: a new work immediately to be published from the pen of the Duchess of Stars!—And the Princess who lends her title to the book is a living portrait of the Princess of Highest Eminence, the Hope of all Civilization.—Orders for copies of THE PRINCESS EGERIA reached the astonished publishers before the book was advertized.

Speaking to editors, Redworth complimented them with friendly intimations of the real authorship of the remarkable work appearing. He used a certain penetrative mildness of tone in saying that 'he hoped the book would succeed': it deserved to; it was original; but the originality might tell against it. All would depend upon a favourable launching of such a book. 'Mrs. Warwick? Mrs. Warwick?' said the most influential of editors, Mr. Marcus Tonans; 'what! that singularly handsome woman?.. The Dannisburgh affair?... She's Whitmonby's heroine. If she writes as cleverly as she talks, her work is worth trumpeting.' He promised to see that it went into good hands for the review, and a prompt review—an essential point; none of your long digestions of the contents.

Diana's indefatigable friend had fair assurances that her book would be noticed before it dropped dead to the public appetite for novelty. He was anxious next, notwithstanding his admiration of the originality of the conception and the cleverness of the writing, lest the Literary Reviews should fail 'to do it justice': he used the term; for if they wounded her, they would take the pleasure out of success; and he had always present to him that picture of the beloved woman kneeling at the fire-grate at The Crossways, which made the thought of her suffering any wound his personal anguish, so crucially sweet and saintly had her image then been stamped on him. He bethought him, in consequence, while sitting in the House of Commons; engaged upon the affairs of the nation, and honestly engaged, for he was a vigilant worker—that the Irish Secretary, Charles Raiser, with whom he stood in amicable relations, had an interest, to the extent of reputed ownership, in the chief of the Literary Reviews. He saw Raiser on the benches, and marked him to speak for him. Looking for him shortly afterward, the man was gone. 'Off to the Opera, if he's not too late for the drop,' a neighbour said, smiling queerly, as though he ought to know; and then Redworth recollected current stories of Raiser's fantastical devotion to the popular prima donna of the angelical voice.—He hurried to the Opera and met the vomit, and heard in the crushroom how divine she had been that night. A fellow member of the House, tolerably intimate with Raiser, informed him, between frightful stomachic roulades of her final aria, of the likeliest place where Raiser might be found when the Opera was over: not at his Club, nor at his chambers: on one of the bridges—Westminster, he fancied.

There was no need for Redworth to run hunting the man at so late an hour, but he was drawn on by the similarity in dissimilarity of this devotee of a woman, who could worship her at a distance, and talk of her to everybody. Not till he beheld Raiser's tall figure cutting the bridge- parapet, with a star over his shoulder, did he reflect on the views the other might entertain of the nocturnal solicitation to see 'justice done' to a lady's new book in a particular Review, and the absurd outside of the request was immediately smothered by the natural simplicity and pressing necessity of its inside.

He crossed the road and said, 'Ah?' in recognition. 'Were you at the Opera this evening?'

'Oh, just at the end,' said Raiser, pacing forward. 'It's a fine night. Did you hear her?'

'No; too late.'

Raiser pressed ahead, to meditate by himself, as was his wont. Finding Redworth beside him, he monologuized in his depths: 'They'll kill her. She puts her soul into it, gives her blood. There's no failing of the voice. You see how it wears her. She's doomed. Half a year's rest on Como . . . somewhere . . . she might be saved! She won't refuse to work.'

'Have you spoken to her?' said Redworth.

'And next to Berlin! Vienna! A horse would be . . . .

I? I don't know her,' Raiser replied. 'Some of their women stand it. She's delicately built. You can't treat a lute like a drum without destroying the instrument. We look on at a murder!'

The haggard prospect from that step of the climax checked his delivery.

Redworth knew him to be a sober man in office, a man with a head for statecraft: he had made a weighty speech in the House a couple of hours back. This Opera cantatrice, no beauty, though gentle, thrilling, winning, was his corner of romance.

'Do you come here often?' he asked.

'Yes, I can't sleep.'

'London at night, from the bridge, looks fine. By the way . . .'

'It's lonely here, that's the advantage,' said Rainer; 'I keep silver in my pocket for poor girls going to their homes, and I'm left in peace. An hour later, there's the dawn down yonder.'

'By the way,' Redworth interposed, and was told that after these nights of her singing she never slept till morning. He swallowed the fact, sympathized, and resumed: 'I want a small favour.'

'No business here, please!'

'Not a bit of it. You know Mrs. Warwick. . . . You know of her. She 's publishing a book. I want you to use your influence to get it noticed quickly, if you can.'

'Warwick? Oh, yes, a handsome woman. Ah, yes; the Dannisburgh affair, yes. What did I hear!—They say she 's thick with Percy Dacier at present. Who was talking of her! Yes, old Lady Dacier. So she 's a friend of yours?'

'She's an old friend,' said Redworth, composing himself; for the dose he had taken was not of the sweetest, and no protestations could be uttered by a man of the world to repel a charge of tattlers. 'The truth is, her book is clever. I have read the proofs. She must have an income, and she won't apply to her husband, and literature should help her, if she 's fairly treated. She 's Irish by descent; Merion's daughter, witty as her father. It's odd you haven't met her. The mere writing of the book is extraordinarily good. If it 's put into capable hands for review! that's all it requires. And full of life . . . bright dialogue . . capital sketches. The book's a piece of literature. Only it must have competent critics!'

So he talked while Rainer ejaculated: 'Warwick? Warwick?' in the irritating tone of dozens of others. 'What did I hear of her husband? He has a post . . . . Yes, yes. Some one said the verdict in that case knocked him over—heart disease, or something.'

He glanced at the dark Thames water. 'Take my word for it, the groves of Academe won't compare with one of our bridges at night, if you seek philosophy. You see the London above and the London below: round us the sleepy city, and the stars in the water looking like souls of suicides. I caught a girl with a bad fit on her once. I had to lecture her! It's when we become parsons we find out our cousinship with these poor peripatetics, whose "last philosophy" is a jump across the parapet. The bridge at night is a bath for a public man. But choose another; leave me mine.'

Redworth took the hint. He stated the title of Mrs. Warwick's book, and imagined from the thoughtful cast of Rainer's head, that he was impressing THE PRINCESS EGERIA On his memory.

Rainer burst out, with clenched fists: 'He beats her! The fellow lives on her and beats her; strikes that woman! He drags her about to every Capital in Europe to make money for him, and the scoundrel pays her with blows.'

In the course of a heavy tirade against the scoundrel, Redworth apprehended that it was the cantatrice's husband. He expressed his horror and regret; paused, and named THE PRINCESS EGERIA and a certain Critical Review. Another outburst seemed to be in preparation. Nothing further was to be done for the book at that hour. So, with a blunt 'Good night,' he left Charles Rainer pacing, and thought on his walk home of the strange effects wrought by women unwittingly upon men (Englishmen); those women, or some of them, as little knowing it as the moon her traditional influence upon the tides. He thought of Percy Dacier too. In his bed he could have wished himself peregrinating a bridge.

The PRINCESS EGERIA appeared, with the reviews at her heels, a pack of clappers, causing her to fly over editions clean as a doe the gates and hedges—to quote Mr. Sullivan Smith, who knew not a sentence of the work save what he gathered of it from Redworth, at their chance meeting on Piccadilly pavement, and then immediately he knew enough to blow his huntsman's horn in honour of the sale. His hallali rang high. 'Here's another Irish girl to win their laurels! 'Tis one of the blazing successes. A most enthralling work, beautifully composed. And where is she now, Mr. Redworth, since she broke away from that husband of hers, that wears the clothes of the worst tailor ever begotten by a thread on a needle, as I tell every soul of 'em in my part of the country?'

'You have seen him?' said Redworth.

'Why, sir, wasn't he on show at the Court he applied to for relief and damages? as we heard when we were watching the case daily, scarce drawing our breath for fear the innocent—and one of our own blood, would be crushed. Sure, there he stood; ay, and looking the very donkey for a woman to flip off her fingers, like the dust from my great uncle's prise of snuff! She's a glory to the old country. And better you than another, I'd say, since it wasn't an Irishman to have her: but what induced the dear lady to take him, is the question we 're all of us asking! And it's mournful to think that somehow you contrive to get the pick of us in the girls! If ever we 're united, 'twill be by a trick of circumvention of that sort, pretty sure. There's a turn in the market when they shut their eyes and drop to the handiest: and

London's a vortex that poor dear dull old Dublin can't compete with. I 'll beg you for the address of the lady her friend, Lady Dunstane.'

Mr. Sullivan Smith walked with Redworth through the park to the House of Commons, discoursing of Rails and his excellent old friend's rise to the top rung of the ladder and Beanstalk land, so elevated that one had to look up at him with watery eyes, as if one had flung a ball at the meridian sun. Arrived at famed St. Stephen's, he sent in his compliments to the noble patriot and accepted an invitation to dinner.

'And mind you read THE PRINCESS EGERIA,' said Redworth.

'Again and again, my friend. The book is bought.' Sullivan Smith slapped his breastpocket.

'There's a bit of Erin in it.'

'It sprouts from Erin.'

'Trumpet it.'

'Loud as cavalry to the charge!'

Once with the title stamped on his memory, the zealous Irishman might be trusted to become an ambulant advertizer. Others, personal friends, adherents, courtiers of Redworth's, were active. Lady Pennon and Henry Wilmers, in the upper circle; Whitmonby and Westlake, in the literary; spread the fever for this new book. The chief interpreter of public opinion caught the way of the wind and headed the gale.

Editions of the book did really run like fires in summer furze; and to such an extent that a simple literary performance grew to be respected in Great Britain, as representing Money.